DIRK WALBRECKER

Translated by Anthea Bell

First published in Germany in 1999 by C. Bertelsmann Jugendbuch Verlag, München

First published in Great Britain in 2000 by Mammoth,
an imprint of Egmont Children's Books Limited,
a division of Egmont Holding Limited
239 Kensington High Street, London W8 6SA

ISBN 0 7497 4156 2

10 9 8 7 6 5 4 3 2 1

A CIP catalogue record for this book is available from the British Library

Typeset by Avon Dataset Ltd, Bidford on Avon, Warwickshire
Printed in Great Britain by Cox & Wyman Ltd, Reading, Berkshire

Contents

One

Greg didn't want today to start.

He didn't want any twittering birds, any dawn light coming through the Venetian blind, or the smell of his school bag, or family breakfast. He didn't want to hear anything. Or see anything. Or smell anything, or say anything. Most of all he didn't want to set eyes on Ben. Or put up with his idiotic remarks.

'Come on, baby brother, admit it! You nicked that cassette from my room! Go on, say it – you fancy Sara too, right? Well, you won't get anywhere there, will you? You've got far too many complexes for that, see, little brother?'

Nicked that cassette. You fancy Sara too. Too many complexes.

Greg would have liked to switch his brain right off. He wanted to wipe out all those horrible things Ben said – but he didn't want to wipe the cassette.

He could feel it under his pillow. He'd listened to it at least ten times, and now he didn't need a Walkman to play it back note by note, word by word.

. . . background music.

I'm recording this specially for you. Do you like me?

. . . background music.

If you do, you'll know the answer to the question you haven't asked me.

. . . background music.

And now I'm asking you the same question!

. . . background music.

Please would you bring your answer to the place where there's something about 250 million years old? It's exactly halfway between your house and mine. It'll be expecting us Saturdays when dark's beginning to fall.

Only then . . . and just you and me.

. . . background music.

A puzzle.

Greg felt his brain working on it, and at the same time something about him felt numb. His body wasn't the same as usual. He couldn't move normally. This wasn't his real body at all!

And his eyes – he wanted to open his eyes and look round him, but they wouldn't open. He was seeing, all the same!

The morning rush was in progress outside his room. Down in the kitchen, his parents were having some kind of argument. Ben chucked something at the wall in the room next to his.

'Hurry up, Greggy, the bathroom's been free for ages!'

Why did Sara give Ben that cassette? Why not me? She looks at me in the bus more often than she looks at him . . . or am I just imagining it?

'Come *on*, Greg! No one's bringing you breakfast in bed!'

Yes. Breakfast. Food, and plenty of it. Greg felt ravenously hungry, and he didn't have the usual sense that his stomach was something empty and round. It felt long, it felt empty and tubular, and it was crying out for . . . for green stuff. Nice green lettuce. Nice green vegetables. Something really, really green.

Someone hammered on Greg's door.

'Look, the school bus isn't doing an extra trip just for you!'

Greg heard Ben's voice only too clearly. He tried to answer, but the words got stuck somewhere on the way. He knew perfectly well it was getting very late. Right now, however, he couldn't care less about the bus and school and all that kerfuffle. Right now nothing interested him but his long, long, empty stomach. He felt an urge to investigate it from the outside and find out what it felt like, but he couldn't even do that. Where he always used to have arms in the normal way . . . there was nothing! Nothing to hold things, nothing he could use to rub his eyes, or rather the apologies for eyes that could dimly make out the room around him, seeing little more than flecks of colour. Eyes? He felt he didn't have just the usual two but a great many more, so that he could see almost the whole way around himself.

I'm still dreaming, okay. It's a dream. All the same, I wish I knew what's the matter with me. So okay, never mind not having arms and hands and proper eyes. I'm going to get up and look in the mirror.

But Greg found he couldn't manage a quick jump out of bed. The usual sensation in his legs simply wasn't there. He had no movable toes, no feet – everything down there seemed vaguely fused together.

'What's the matter with Greg? Does his class start school late today?'

'Well, I'm not waiting for my little brother any longer.'

Greg didn't feel particularly little, but at the moment he wasn't interested in the problem bothering Pa and Ben. He had enough to occupy his mind, wondering about himself and his extremely peculiar shape. To his great surprise, it seemed he could move very well even without the usual extremities. Almost of their own accord, gentle wavy movements began running through his body. They began at the far end, moved up through his long, empty stomach and all the way to his head . . . he made them very smoothly, and with an unusual sense of well-being. Then Greg made another surprising discovery: somewhere around the place where he didn't have arms, things were moving all the same. Not just two of them, but six! They were short and they had no joints, but he could move them: not singly, only in pairs. They were nothing like as – well, as handy as hands, but they obviously had their uses. And the harder Greg concentrated on these new physical sensations, the more discoveries he made. There were several movable items down on the lower part of his long body too – rather short, stumpy excrescences arranged in pairs, two of them at the very far end.

Greg tried counting, but he wasn't sure: sometimes he thought he had twelve of these excrescences, another time he made it as many as sixteen.

Then he gave up counting, because other things were happening in the house. The front door slammed twice in quick succession. Footsteps hurried up the stairs, and he heard the door handle being rattled.

'Greg, do wake up! What's the matter? You never usually lock your door! Open it this minute!'

This was getting complicated. Look at it one way, and Greg was feeling quite at home in his peculiar new physical state. Look at it another, and he was in real trouble with his mother. It was true, he really had locked his bedroom door last night, for the first time in his life. And he had no earthly reason to stay in bed any longer. School had to begin some time. School . . . well, that was a joke in the circumstances!

'Greg, for the last time, come out! I'm getting seriously worried. Can you hear me?'

'Yyyyeee . . .'

It wasn't a real yes, more of a gurgle, a long-drawn-out sound, breathed rather than spoken. It seemed to stick in Greg's throat.

Throat? Something was wrong there too: not only could Greg easily turn his head far to the left and the right, but thanks to some extraordinary mechanism that he couldn't quite control yet, he could draw it almost all the way down into his body.

Suddenly this was all too much for Greg. It was not being able to speak that really made him panic-stricken.

'Greg, dear, I can't hear you! Speak up!'

'Yyyy . . . yeee . . .'

Greg gave up. He was never going to cope with the

situation this way. He heard his mother come running upstairs to – to do goodness knew what. He was feeling worried about her. He knew her poor nerves only too well. She wasn't used to getting such surprises from him.

What could he do? How could he cope with the situation? Where was there an escape route? Ma's going to get a terrible shock if she sees me like this, he thought. And even if it's all my imagination and I look the same as usual to her, that's going to be awkward enough.

At least his brain was still working. That was a comfort. Something else was working too, and better than ever: his hearing. It was as if he'd had a highly sensitive bug implanted in him, picking up a huge range of high and low frequencies. Greg knew about creatures with extra-good hearing from all his studies of wildlife. He was very interested in the animal kingdom.

Animal kingdom? But how . . .? Greg forced himself not to follow this absurd train of thought any further for the moment.

Hoping to get a better grip on the situation, he decided to concentrate entirely on ways of moving. To his surprise he found he could do something that was quite fun: even lying down, he could bend and bend until one end of his body reached the other. He could also coil up. When he coiled up something tickled his sides quite pleasantly. Something sharp and bristly, or hairy.

Okay, now I'm going to get off this bed, Greg decided. Promptly and almost automatically, those footlike or leglike things began to move, reaching first all the way back and then all the way forward, moving in neat pairs. Lying on his front, he had only to turn his entire body a little way and then he really could get off the bed, step by step and with some agility, or anyway without too much strain.

And as Greg was crawling over the floor, the awful truth suddenly occurred to him: I'm a caterpillar. That's what it is, no two ways about it, I'm a caterpillar! A giant caterpillar!

Extraordinary and incredible as this notion was, Greg had no time to get accustomed to it now. His excellent hearing had picked up the sound of his mother approaching from an unusual angle. First there was a grunt. Then a clattering sound on the outside wall of the house. Then cautious steps coming up a ladder. And then a dark shadow appeared on the other side of the Venetian blind. Greg heard her breathing. He also, surprisingly, registered something else: he had picked up his mother's sense of agitation and alarm.

The window wasn't latched. She had only to make one movement.

'Greg?'

Once again, Greg tried to make something like a human sound.

'Yyyy . . .'

'Greg, dear?'

Greg lay motionless on the floor, stretched full length. He gazed helplessly at the window. A shadowy something pushed the slats of the blind apart. A broad strip of bright morning light fell straight on Greg, dazzling him.

'Nooooo!'

His mother's scream was so strange and upsetting that Greg began to tremble. Involuntarily, he turned away from the window. Once again his back pair of legs began to move, then the next pair took up the movement, and the next and the next, and so on, until it reached the front. With surprising speed and agility, Greg crawled under his bed.

Oh, for some peace and quiet! He didn't want to hear anything else that was going on outside. He just wanted to concentrate on himself and try to understand what this was all about. It wasn't the first time he'd taken refuge under this bed. He'd dived underneath it several times since they moved in two months ago, to hide the comic drawings he did. Sketches and a few completed pictures – a crab and a scorpion, both rather shy, meeting and falling in love. Not for the eyes of brothers snooping around or mothers bent on tidying up. Greg also had a bag of jelly babies and two chocolate bars stashed under the bed. He could smell them only too clearly, and instantly he felt hungry again. Ravenously hungry. He could hardly bear it.

I know what I'll do, Greg told himself, I'll let the feeling spread right through my body and then do an experiment. I'll analyse myself. Me: Gregor Hansen, son of Thomas Hansen, architect, and Helen Hansen, student of alternative medicine. He's not at school this Tuesday morning, he's lying under his bed instead. There are good reasons why he's taken refuge there. First, that unpleasant business with his brother, Ben. Second, a certain Sara Auster, who lives in a house in the country, like the Hansen family, and who takes the same bus to school almost every morning. So this Sara Auster . . .

Greg was finding it difficult to concentrate. He felt dizzy, and the smell of chocolate so close nauseated him. With the last of his strength, Greg tried to complete his experiment.

The aforesaid Greg Hansen, up till now obviously human, I repeat, human – the aforesaid Greg Hansen hasn't had any breakfast yet, so not surprisingly he feels as if he's mutated into a half-starved, ravenous giant caterpillar. So he is now about to remutate as follows:

Greg Hansen will crawl out from under his bed on all fours – definitely just on all fours. He will stand up on his two legs – only two legs, remember! – he will open the door, leave his room, go into the bathroom, clean his teeth, and then ask his mother for a double helping of breakfast.

Once again a sense of dizziness swept through Greg's head. Dazed, he crawled out from under the bed. The crawling movement began at the far end and ran right through his body in waves until it reached the front.

Now then, Greg told himself trying to remutate, stand up, go over to the door and open it!

It didn't work.

From a distance, and yet she sounded quite close, he could hear his mother on the mobile phone.

'Come home at once, Thomas! Never mind the digger! Never mind the client! Never mind anything. If you don't come home straight away I'll have to raise the alarm with someone else!'

Greg didn't want to listen to this. He'd have liked to cover his ears with his non-existent hands. All he wanted was to be alone and to forget everything around him. He crawled over to his bed in the corner, effortlessly raised the front of his body, slithered on to the mattress with a gentle movement and coiled up – exactly like a caterpillar.

* * *

How long he lay like that Greg didn't know. His usually reliable sense of time let him down. It was his father's voice that brought him back to the present.

'You're suffering from delusions, darling.'

'See for yourself, Thomas!'

'Look, if I break the door down it'll cost a mint of money to get it repaired.'

The cassette! A shock ran through Greg's caterpillar body, and his brain reacted just like yesterday: it'll be a disaster if they discover that cassette and Ben finds out.

Then something happened that was outside Greg's control. Two small and extremely mobile feelers on top of his head, two feelers apparently with ideas of their own and working on instinct, searched under his pillow for the mini-cassette. A strange need to bite something came over Greg. He grabbed the cassette in his jaws and began shredding the plastic case. It hurt, it tasted disgusting, and Greg was breathing stertorously.

At that moment there was a mighty crash: Mr Hansen had broken the door down and was now standing with his wife in the splintered door frame.

Everything was quiet. Uncannily quiet.

Greg lay there motionless. His parents didn't move either.

Ma can't make it out at all. Ma is so horrified she's

going to faint any moment now, Greg sensed, although he didn't understand how he could pick all that up without seeing her.

Sure enough, she whispered, 'Help – I feel faint!' Then it was quiet again.

What's Pa thinking? Greg wondered. What's going through *his* mind? But he couldn't read his father's thoughts any better than usual.

Out in the garden the birds were twittering, and Greg's stomach was rumbling.

'But where's Greg?' whispered Mr Hansen. His voice was husky.

Very slowly, Greg turned his head towards the door.

'Watch out!' he heard his father whisper, contradicting himself next minute: 'There's nothing to be frightened of. It looks harmless.'

Greg wanted to say: Fetch me something to eat! He tried getting the idea across by rearing up the front of his body.

'Look at those eyes!' whispered Mrs Hansen.

'They're not real!' said Mr Hansen, brusquely. 'They're only for show – to scare off predators. It's camouflage.'

'What are we going to do?'

'Ask me another!'

Greg felt bad. As usual when everyone was quiet

and nobody did anything, he felt awkward, as if the whole situation was his fault.

He'd have liked to say: It'll be all right.

But for one thing, no such way of communicating was open to him and, for another, there was nothing to suggest that it *would* be all right. Instead, Greg felt horribly sick. The pieces of cassette seemed to be indigestible. They'd stuck somewhere near his front end – where he still had the remnants of a throatlike feeling. I'm going to throw up, he thought. He felt an urgent need to get away somewhere, somehow, out of his parents' sight. They themselves seemed to be rooted to the spot, staring at the caterpillar creature as if it were an extra-terrestrial.

Ma's thoughts came through to Greg loud and clear, right into his head, as if he had a decoding device implanted in it: she was wishing all this would stop, at once, without any fuss. Pa's thoughts were harder to decode, but he conveyed something between fury and bafflement, and he was still at a loss for words.

Hoping to cope with the nausea – it was getting worse and worse – Greg decided to crawl under his desk.

'Look!' he heard his mother's voice. It sounded odd but emotional.

Oh, go away, Greg would have liked to tell them, go

away and leave me alone! But he could make no sound except for a few gurgles. He tried coiling up again, and his parents actually seemed to take this as a sign that they *should* go away. Greg thought he heard them putting a makeshift barricade over the doorway.

Exhausted and tormented by stomachache and hunger, Greg lapsed into a kind of unconsciousness.

Two

When Greg woke up again he was all confused. He'd just done the school bus journey, and everything had been the same as usual.

Ben was at the stop ahead of him. Standing next to Sara, of course, and acting all macho. Talking big, making showy gestures like an actor. Producing charming smiles and pulling silly faces. And when he got into the bus he held Sara's arm as if he'd just taken a special course in charming the birds out of the trees.

Ben and Sara at the front of the bus. So who was right at the back, as usual, with his heart thudding? Greg, of course.

Now for the famous, cunning trick of making out you see something fascinating on the other side of the window, but you're really looking for something much more fascinating *in* the window.

Maybe he could meet her eyes, just for a moment.

For once, Ben wasn't rabbiting on, and Sara was looking out of the bus window too. Or was she? Her eyes didn't move; they kept staring at the glass. Angles of incidence and reflection ... Anyway, not looking into space, no, looking straight at me – very intently. Can't hold her gaze for very long.

The bus starts – it's off ...

Then, suddenly, Ben's voice up close, no mistaking him. 'Are you taking the mickey or what?'

And Pa's voice: 'Wait a minute ...'

Then Ma's voice: 'Better not say anything just now.'

Greg was wide awake. Also, he was coiled up and he felt sick.

'I don't believe this. I reckon I'm at the movies,' said Ben. His voice sounded curiously husky as it came to Greg's ears.

Then Greg retched. All the many segments of his body began to shiver. He had to stretch out full length. A stertorous sound came from the thing resembling a mouth at his front end. Then, with a couple of violent convulsions, he brought up splinters and bits of audiocassette.

'He's not well! He needs help!'

Greg heard his mother's voice, full of concern, followed by Ben's and his father's.

'I don't believe it!'

17

'I don't believe it either!'

The three of them had drawn closer together.

'But that . . .' began Ma, and Greg sensed her confusion.

'That's the remains of an audiocassette. No doubt about it,' remarked Mr Hansen.

Ben said nothing, but Greg was extremely conscious of him. As usual, he wanted to run away or hide. In spite of the peculiar things that had happened, he felt his conscience pricking him again. He was scared, too, scared Ben would be angry and, most of all, scared that he'd take revenge.

Greg felt better now he'd thrown up, but he also felt hungry again – hungrier than ever. He'd just love a mouthful of something, preferably something green.

'He's hungry. He isn't feeling well,' said Mrs Hansen. 'We must do something for him!'

'Like what?'

'Yes, like what?'

There was a brief discussion. Ben, although he protested indignantly, was sent to fetch a cloth to mop up after Greg. And whether he liked it or not, Pa was dispatched to find something edible.

Greg tried to switch off and blank out the whole conversation. He felt as if he'd heard all this yesterday, and through all the days, months and years before yesterday. The next development wasn't unfamiliar either: once Ben had cleaned the floor in front of the desk, moaning and groaning about it, Mrs Hansen came back with two little bottles.

'Come on, dear, you need some drops for the shock. Rescue Remedy is sure to do you good. And after that we can try Olive.'

Greg put up with this demonstration of motherly love in the form of Bach Flower Remedies dripped into his mouth opening. It wasn't the first time. Ma sounded as if she were talking to a ten-year-old, but there was something in her voice that made Greg uncomfortable. He felt like crawling right away from it.

Then, at last, food arrived. Greg smelled it coming up the stairs. Lettuces. Lovely lettuces. Mr Hansen handed them in distrustfully, shaking his head. All this was too much for him.

'Here you are.'

'Call him Greg, can't you?'

Mr Hansen raised his voice. 'That's not Gregor. It's a – it's some kind of *creature*. This is a nightmare!'

Greg paid no attention to this discussion. He was busy gulping lettuce. Leaf after leaf of lettuce, with an expertise that surprised him. He heard his jaws crunching slightly, a strange but extremely satisfying noise. And as he chewed and crunched he discovered something interesting about his appearance, thanks to Ben.

'Why's it got that funny little red horn down the far end? Doesn't match its dark grey skin. And just look at those jaws! I mean, this is some kind of monster! It's horrible!'

Greg felt like saying, 'Look at yourself, then, why don't you?' It was just the same as before this peculiar transformation: he couldn't cope with Ben. Didn't know how to defend himself. The kind of support he was likely to get from other quarters sounded the same as usual too.

'Don't exaggerate, Ben,' said Pa, in his usual mild tones. Ma was more sympathetic.

'How can you talk like that, Ben? Never mind *what* it is – all living creatures can pick up vibrations.'

'Okay, okay, I've got nothing against animals. I just feel kind of stressed. Look, I have to go and phone my mates.'

'Oh no, you don't!'

Greg was surprised. Pa seldom contradicted Ben so firmly.

'No one's saying a word about this to anyone outside. Not a word! We'd be certified insane!'

All of a sudden everything was perfectly quiet. Greg had eaten both lettuces down to the last bit of stalk, and

Mrs Hansen seemed to have issued some unspoken demand for silence.

'Okay, okay,' muttered Ben.

'Okay,' Mr Hansen confirmed.

And the three of them left the room without any further remarks, putting a makeshift barrier across the doorway again. Greg was alone. Out on the stairs, he could hear them drawing up a new set of house rules.

'Not a word, understand? Not at school, not any-where else. Not to the neighbours, not to friends and family. And Grandfather mustn't hear about it either. What we'd better do . . .' Then the living-room door was opened downstairs. Mr Hansen was still talking, and Greg could tell that his mother and Ben were managing to get a word in now and then, but it was as if it all reached him through a badly-tuned radio trans-mitter. Apart from which, just now Greg was more interested in himself than them.

He didn't feel as if he'd had anywhere near enough to eat, but there were other things he wanted to do. This strange body with all its different possible ways of moving was most intriguing. Just to experiment, he began turning and coiling, raising and lowering his head, and doing that funny thing with it again – drawing it right in so that it seemed to disappear. It made Greg feel safe, protected. He was aware of the little horn Ben had mentioned, too – a strange part of him, and he couldn't even touch or feel it, the way he used to be able to touch his whole body. Yet it was clearly there, obviously for some purpose. Anyway, everything down below was different, although just now that didn't interest Greg so much. He was concentrating on getting to know more about his amazing sensations of movement: all these leglike things were fascinating. Suddenly he wanted to climb. Like a genuine caterpillar – was he or wasn't he a genuine caterpillar? – he wanted to try the apparently impossible: he wanted to climb walls. And then crawl along the ceiling! Life from above would probably look quite different.

This creepy-crawly venture turned out to be good fun. For the first time ever, Greg could look down on his room from a dizzy height – not that he felt dizzy himself, and he knew he was in very little danger of falling. There was some kind of sticky sucker device on his hind feet, and it was only when he tried to move too fast that he seemed to risk taking a dive. Two pairs of legs at least had to have a good grip on a surface at the same time. The rest of his long body could do more or less as it liked: expand or contract, rear up or turn right round. It didn't feel dangerous except near the ceiling light, where Greg's sensitive feelings told him about the electric waves coming his way. They seemed to have a numbing effect.

Pity I can't see better, thought Greg regretfully. He was still confused by his inability to make out much except colours and shapes, but at the same time he could see in several directions at once, and at very wide angles . . .

Then the peaceful atmosphere was rudely shattered. The door was opened, and there stood Mr and Mrs Hansen in his room.

Silence. Astonished silence.

'Where on earth is he?'

Steps. Movement. Uneven breathing.

'I don't believe it!'

Greg didn't move. He was rather enjoying this.

'But we made sure the door was . . .'

'He isn't under the bed . . .'

And then his mother's shriek, 'There!'

'Don't scare me like that!'

Greg wasn't sure if this was meant for him or Ma.

'Come down from there this minute!'

Well, that sounded like real life. Here Greg did something he'd never normally have dared to do: he offered passive resistance, and clung stubbornly to the ceiling.

'Now what? What are we going to do?'

At this point something happened that embarrassed Greg deeply: all of a sudden he needed to go to the lavatory, but in a brand-new way. The physical process seemed to be outside his control. He felt some kind of opening mechanism move at his back end, there was a brief convulsion, and a sense of relief. Then a plop, and something not exactly small but round, black and shiny landed at his parents' feet.

'For heaven's sake!' Mr Hansen protested.

At the same time Greg heard his brother. 'What a load of rubbish! Typical!'

'Don't be so stupid!' snapped Mr Hansen. 'Go and get a bucket and a cloth!'

'Why does it always have to be me?'

Greg could neither grin nor laugh, but in spite of his awkward situation he did feel a certain malicious pleasure. He enjoyed that, and it didn't do any harm.

'Look, wouldn't you like to come down from there?'

That was Ma trying gentle persuasion, same as usual, and Greg did feel he couldn't stay upside-down for ever. Particularly since his involuntary evacuation just now had left him feeling empty inside. He needed to eat again.

'It's a mirage, that's what it is. I mean, this can't be true! What have we done to have a thing like this creep into our house?' Mr Hansen's nerves seemed to be stretched to breaking point. Greg heard him sit down on his, Greg's, bed and groan several times running.

'I told you all along there were bad vibrations in this house. I wanted an exorcism ceremony, but you wouldn't listen to me, Thomas.'

'Oh, *get* the place exorcised if you want. Get it exorcised of all its bad vibrations *and* that creature up there!'

Greg felt a pang – somewhere deep inside, a feeling that had become familiar to him these last few months.

'You know, I can't help thinking about all those wildlife films of his,' said Mrs Hansen quietly. 'He's been addicted to them for years! Just look at that stack of videos.'

'Oh, stop it. None of this makes any sense. It's not Greg we're talking about, we're talking about that thing up there. None of this is real, anyway. Surreal, that's what it is. Pure delusion.'

'Tell you what, this is the third millennium!' said Ben. 'We've got it right here in our house. The third millennium exclusive, live. Throwing up and who knows what else!'

Here Greg found that he couldn't keep clinging to the ceiling for ever. There was a rumbling inside him, and his back pair of legs urged him to get down on the floor again as soon as he possibly could.

At that moment Mr Hansen's mobile phone rang.

'Yes?'

Even before Pa began talking Greg knew the caller was his grandfather.

'Yes, yes, we're fine ... all a bit hectic at the moment ... Yes, my building projects, very stressful ... Helen? Oh, she's okay ... well, her mind's rather occupied – her exams, you know ... I mean, taking up something new so late in life ... Ben? No idea ... oh, yes, he's out a good deal these days, could be in love, sure, but you don't mention that in the bosom of your family ... Yes, we spend a good deal of time together on the computer ... Gregor? Oh, well, Greg ... well, you know Greg. I mean, we've all been through the awkward stage ... All very well for you to laugh! No, not yet, I'm afraid ... No, unfortunately we'll have to postpone it for a bit ... Look, Helen will explain it all to you herself ... No, no, it's because of Greg – the thing is, you see, Greg's not well ... Quite suddenly, over-night, you might say ... could be infectious ... No, certainly not, not in any circumstances! It must be some kind of virus ... No, you know Helen's dead-set against conventional medicine, she'd rather deal with it herself ... No, Paul, look, I'm telling you it's impossible ... Oh yes, everything else is going according to plan ... Yes, we've got your room ready, all it needs now is the special bed . . . Listen, I have to ring off now. There's a client just arrived . . . No, at the moment Helen's with the . . . with Greg. She'll call you back . . . See you!'

A long, heartfelt sigh of relief.

Meanwhile, Greg had landed on the floor safe and sound, but something else was suddenly bothering him. It wasn't just that he felt hungry again. Most of all, he needed to be alone. Once again, it was Ma who seemed to read his mind.

'Let's go downstairs. Maybe he needs to sleep. And if you ask me . . .'

Greg wasn't listening to what his father and Ben had to say any more. All of a sudden he saw his grandfather standing there as vividly as if he were real: Grandfather's back was bent, but you got a sense of something strong and powerful inside him. Grandfather, with that mischievous twinkle in his eyes. There was sometimes an absent, dreamy look in those eyes. He was grey haired, and usually rather grey faced too these days. Greg felt very sad when he thought about his grandfather – his metamorphosis had made no difference to that. He loved him, he'd been delighted to hear that Grandfather was moving in with them. And now it seemed Grandfather couldn't come after all, and all because of him! Why doesn't Pa just tell him what's happened, thought Greg, why the big cover-up?

It was as if Greg's sense of time had been switched off again. At some point he realised everything around him was much darker. He still wanted food, but he'd found out that if he kept still he didn't feel so hungry. Instead, he was overwhelmed by a kind of melancholy. No concrete thoughts. No real conscious existence any more. Everything was inside him, filling him with sadness. Memories of words mixed in with these feelings. Words he'd bitten back. Words he couldn't say now. He could only think them, dream them.

It must have been late in the evening when his mother came into the room and Greg woke up. He was lying coiled up under his desk, not moving. He didn't know whether he wanted a visitor or not.

'Greggy?'

Greg sensed his mother approaching, almost without a sound. She crouched down on the floor beside him.

'Greggy, can you hear me? Are you awake?'

Greg didn't react.

'Do you need anything, Greggy? Would you like me to bring you something?'

An odd idea came into Greg's mind: why's she calling me by my name? How is she so sure it's really me? I'm not even sure of it myself.

'Can you hear my voice, Greg? It's me, your ... your ...'

Mrs Hansen stopped. Greg could sense exactly what was going on inside her. She wasn't sure. She wasn't really sure, but she was trying to suppress her doubts. She wanted to sound like his mother, and she was wishing urgently, with almost magical energy, for the creature in front of her to be her child. Or become her child again.

'Greg, what's the matter with you? Do you need help?'

Greg stayed where he was, not moving – tense, but in a way he was quite enjoying the situation. He could hear every sound, every word, more clearly than he'd ever heard things before. And the fascinating thing was that in between the sounds he heard words that hadn't been spoken aloud at all. They were saying: please, please, please!

His mother thought that one word, 'please', over and over again. It made its way right into Greg. There wasn't a thing he could do to keep it out.

Come to think of it, this experience wasn't entirely new. He'd quite often felt as if he could read thoughts, although only with a few people. It worked with Ma, like now, and it sometimes worked with Grandfather.

And with the person he'd been trying to get close to for the last few weeks – he felt sure he could do it with her but unfortunately he had no proof.

'Greg, do please show that you can understand me – try to show me somehow!'

Greg hesitated. In one way this was a very pleasing situation. But there was something so warm in Ma's voice, such a pleading note, that in the end his caterpillar body moved almost of its own accord.

'Listen, I want to help you. I want to understand what's happened!'

Greg would very much have liked to say, 'Me too!' He stretched slightly, and it was quite nice to feel his mother's hand stroking his back very, very gently.

Yet Greg didn't really like it either. He turned slightly to one side, so that his mother was stroking the hairs along his body, and she involuntarily snatched her hand back as if she'd touched a stinging nettle. Almost at the same time, even though she didn't utter them aloud, Greg picked up the words:

'It's him all right! He reacts just the same as usual!'

It seemed that this observation had calmed Ma down. She was sitting on the floor in silence now, not moving. Her gaze rested on the caterpillar's body, but it was trying to look inside him at the same time. Her breathing was regular and very slow.

'Please, please!' She went on transmitting that 'please', at long intervals and without any distress in her tone.

All the same, Greg felt pressurised.

He transmitted his own wishes back. Please go away! You could go and get me something to eat, but do please leave me alone!

To Greg's surprise, Mrs Hansen stood up and left the room without a word. But she obviously hadn't registered his request for more food.

I'll have to see about that for myself, thought Greg. He waited until the whispering in his parents' bedroom died down, and all he could hear was Pa snoring. The idea of leaving his room in the middle of the night made his heart beat fast.

But somehow I seem to know how to do it, thought Greg rather fretfully, trying to use his feelers: stretch out ... pull in ... stretch out again. Bend, curve, stretch as far up as I can go ... it was all rather strange and unfamiliar, but he'd soon get the hang of it.

Greg started moving. He knew where he was going. He had to get downstairs and find something edible. He also wanted to try out some more ways of getting around, and although it was long past midnight, Greg felt as perky as if it were midday. A thought came into his mind: Suppose I turned up in Ben's doorway now?

NO ENTRY! KEEP OUT! He could see that un-welcoming notice Ben had put up only too clearly in his mind's eye.

I could tear it down, I could crunch it up, I could munch the very last little bit of it . . .

But the idea made Greg feel sick. He didn't dare. Go on, get downstairs, his empty stomach told him. Greg obeyed it. Step by step, carefully making his way forward without any sound at all, he moved in the direction of the stairs – and then stopped. It wasn't the dark that bothered him. He just couldn't get his mind around having to stand on six or seven steps at once.

Okay, one at a time, then. Move up and down again, on all fourteen legs! And again. Up and down again. Gregor the giant caterpillar could get quite addicted to stairs.

Then, at last, Greg was standing – or rather lying – at the larder door.

Now what?

Greg wished he didn't have a guilty conscience over nocturnal raids on the larder. And all the different smells confused him. Also, he suddenly felt very small again – pathetically small!

But when he raised and stretched his front segments he felt better. No difficulty about opening the door, and then he knew what to do. Eat. Eat. Keep on eating!

Greg started on the vegetables. White cabbage and Chinese cabbage. Endives and lettuce. Green carrot tops, and a bit of fennel, and a leek just to round things off. Greg's taste buds were going wild, but never mind: he was all caterpillar, he had to eat and eat and eat, and never mind the consequences!

Now a good hearty belch. Then a constitutional – a few times round the living-room floor. Then another belch. Then a virtuoso climbing display, from the new leather sofa over the stereo and the TV set, and right into the trough of flowering plants in the conservatory area. Now some fresh Alpine violets and a couple of delicious primulas for afters – well, it's their own fault for letting me practically starve to death!

After that, Greg wanted to be back in his own room. He did the now familiar stair-climbing trick, and passed that mean, nasty notice. One final belch right outside Ben's room. Greg felt really good.

Next morning, chaos reigned in the Hansen household. Greg was awake first, because he felt he had to obey the call of nature, urgently. Then Mrs Hansen lost her cool. The sight of the raided larder and the nibbled house-plants made it very clear that she had underestimated her mutated son's appetite. Next it was Mr Hansen's turn to panic. He had just been making sure –

surreptitiously, but not unobserved – that Greg was still alive, when the doorbell rang.

'Ssh!' hissed Pa. Even Greg could hear it. There was deathly silence for a couple of seconds. Then the bell rang again, loud and long.

'It's Grandfather's special bed!' whispered Greg's mother.

Why a caterpillar should feel impelled to leave its room just at this delicate moment didn't become clear until later, but Greg's appearance sent the master of the house into a frenzy. Waving his hands and feet about, he tried to keep Greg back. Once again Mrs Hansen tried to protect her child. *Child*? With great determination she set about preventing her husband from doing anything he might regret. Downstairs there was a loud, insistent hammering at the door. Whoever was there seemed very certain there'd be someone at home.

'Want me to sort it out?' whispered Ben, grinning.

His intervention wasn't called for. Soon afterwards, there was a sound of rattling and clattering, a large item of furniture was deposited outside the front door to the sound of cursing, and an envelope dropped through the letter-box.

None of this bothered Greg. He had other needs, and they were making themselves felt at the far end of his body. He would have liked to get to the lavatory, or some other private place. He'd have liked that very much indeed. But the lavatory door was closed, and no one realised how desperate he was.

A plopping sound again, and there lay something large, round, black and shiny in the middle of the landing.

'Oh, this is too much!' said Mr Hansen. He really meant the men simply leaving the bed outside the house and going away.

'You can say that again!' said Ben, indicating the shiny black offering. 'Well, someone else can deal with it this time. I have to catch the school bus!'

The bus!

Greg didn't know which was worse, his embarrassment at what he'd just done, or the memory of a certain Sara Auster. Never mind. He went back into his room. He didn't want to hear any more about anything at all.

Greg's wish for peace and quiet was not granted. After the Hansen family had gulped its breakfast downstairs, his father reappeared with various tools. Hammering, drilling, swearing and getting all sticky with glue, he set to work on the door frame. He had no idea how painful every sound he made was to Greg, and how unpleasantly pungent he found the smell of glue. It seemed to crawl all over his body.

Greg suddenly wanted to turn and appeal to his father: Please tell me what's wrong with me!

But his father didn't notice. He just went on hammering away, making a frightful noise, and he didn't go into Greg's room until the door and the lock were back in working order. He stopped beside the desk – just as he always did when Greg was doing his homework in the evening.

Now what? Greg wondered. He didn't expect a very positive answer.

Instead, all was quiet – quiet for a very long time. Mr Hansen just stood there in silence, staring down at the creature that was supposed to be his son, shaking his head very slightly now and then, and obviously thinking hard.

Greg couldn't guess his thoughts.

Greg's parents held a council of war at midday. Ma had been out of the house briefly, and Pa had called the office to say he wouldn't be coming in. Now they were both sitting in the living-room. Greg could hear only fragments of their conversation.

'Getting outside help' was the first subject under discussion: no, no – impossible, absolutely impossible ... the shame of it ... the neighbours ... under no circumstances ... they'll think we're crazy ...

extraordinary phenomenon . . . nothing short of a catastrophe . . .

Oh yes, Greg wondered, who for?

'Grandfather' was next on the agenda: urgent need of nursing care . . . mustn't agitate an old man like that . . . right way to behave, it's our duty . . . come to some kind of decision soon . . .

Oh, Greg wished, do let him come!

Next came that perennial topic 'School': how do we get a medical certificate . . . just say he's leaving? . . . can't ask Ben to keep the pretence up . . . hasn't made friends there yet, luckily . . . we could say it's a case of psychomotor disturbance . . .

What on earth do they mean by that? wondered Greg.

The final item on the agenda was 'The care and nutrition of domestic pets', and here the discussion became loud and heated: draw up some plan of action . . . insatiable appetite . . . . . . responsibility . . . healthy diet . . . no exercise area . . . sheer insanity . . . positive disaster . . .

And all because of me, thought Greg, feeling a little bit smug about it.

Soon after that Ben came home – you couldn't miss hearing him. He was in high spirits, and he brought news.

'The Austers want to meet their new neighbours. They've suggested a family get-together next weekend.'

Greg could hear every word. His whole body was shaken by feelings he'd known only in the last few weeks.

Sara.

It had happened right after their first meeting in the morning at the bus stop. Flash! It was her eyes at first, those big, big eyes. He'd really only looked straight into them that one time, and afterwards he kept asking himself how something so brief could catapult you into another dimension. Was she teasing him? Was it enticement? Some kind of game?

What exactly had he seen in her eyes? A friendly look? Yes. An affectionate look? Oh, yes. But something very sad too, or melancholy, or lonely.

After that he didn't trust himself any more. Nor, obviously, did Sara trust herself either. They'd even avoided standing next to each other at the bus stop, or in the bus, or getting out of the bus together. Their eyes had met a few times only from a distance, or in the window-pane, when they locked briefly, and then . . . Such an anxious feeling, but what about?

Why does looking at each other make you feel all anxious? Why does that one glance linger long after you're in your English lesson or the lab, looking at the computer screen or hanging from a rope in the gym –

why there? A glance going right through you, making you feel all excited?

Does Sara feel the same? Did she see me looking at her the same way? Does she go to sleep thinking of it too, not wanting any other ideas to blot it out?

Or was it just that one time?

Why did she give that cassette to Ben, of all people? What does she want him to do? What does she want to ask him?

Why's it always Ben? Why him? How does he manage to act so relaxed? Bragging, cracking jokes, grinning and laughing fit for two Bens at once, if not more. And no one dares contradict him. It was like that in our old school, and it's just the same in this new one.

Once again, Greg had lost all sense of time and reality. He was lying coiled up, with his head drawn in, when he suddenly felt a dull pain in his side.

'Hey, creepy-crawly, don't just lie about like that! Want me to tell you something?'

Greg made no move to abandon his protective attitude.

'No need to act so insulted, little one! And what's that thingummy on your backside?'

Greg felt something grab him at a very sensitive spot. He reacted in a way he couldn't control.

'Ouch! What's the idea, you filthy brute?'

Greg didn't move. He heard his parents come running upstairs.

'What's the matter? Did he attack you?'

'What are you doing to him?'

His parents were in the room. Head drawn in, but wide awake all the same, Greg observed everything that was going on around him.

'It hurts like hell!' Ben complained. 'He just tried to poison me. It stinks, too. Yuk!'

'There's some calamine lotion in the bathroom cupboard.'

'Helen, surely you can see we can't go on like this!' said Mr Hansen in a husky voice. 'It's dangerous!'

'Don't exaggerate so, Thomas!'

'The creature's unpredictable . . .'

Unpredictable, Greg would have liked to say, you bet your life!

He still felt safe in his coiled-up position, but he felt cowardly too. In fact he felt very cowardly. He longed to make his escape. At the same time he wanted to see this situation through.

Most of all, he didn't want to claim victory. Whatever that thing was at the back of him, it seemed to have its uses – but Greg would rather defend himself some other way.

Not that that was much use.

Greg wondered about his father. As soon as Ben came back with his hand ostentatiously bandaged, Pa started on what amounted to an interrogation: 'Now then, Ben, I want you to tell me what's been going on between the pair of you recently!'

Greg listened intently. His brother took his time over answering.

'Why ask that now?'

'Answer me, please!'

'Nothing special. Just harmless squabbling.'

'And when you were yelling at Gregor the other evening, what was all that about?'

'Nothing. Usual sort of territorial competition, I suppose.'

'Have you noticed anything about Greg recently?'

'Nope, only that he's growing up. Typical changes of puberty.'

Something rumbled inside Greg. He couldn't keep his protective attitude up any more. His head shot out of its wrappings of skin, and the front segments of his body reared into the air.

'Careful!' cried Mr Hansen in alarm.

'Anyway, that's not Greg, that's some kind of monster!' cried Ben.

'Oh, do stop it!' Mrs Hansen begged them.

Greg noticed that all three of them were suddenly in a great hurry to leave his room and lock the door.

The next few days passed relatively quietly, apart from a few minor hiccups. Greg was concentrating on himself and his new body. He'd come to terms with it for the time being. Most of what went on inside his head was much the same as before he changed shape, but everything else was a biological mystery – although quite an intriguing one sometimes, as he was finding out.

Of course his first thought every time he woke up was to check his extremities. Can I still grab something? How many legs do I need for standing and walking? Next he had to test his eyesight. Can I see clearly again, or do I still have that peculiar soft-focus panoramic vision?

Well, Greg said to himself, so what? There've been worse catastrophes and weirder things happen in the world. I'm not letting this get me down in a hurry – not as my real self and not as a caterpillar either.

Then he turned his attention to his school equipment. First he began gleefully nibbling his exercise books, files and textbooks, then he crunched them up with relish. But he was very careful not to eat anything indigestible, because that cassette, or rather the words on the cassette, still lay as heavy as ever on his stomach.

Greg had reached a compromise on his need to go to the lavatory several times a day. He did feel increasingly inclined just to do it wherever he happened to be crawling or climbing at the time. On the other hand, he wanted to show his mother some consideration, and she'd made him a kind of caterpillar toilet in a corner of the room. It was not unlike a cat's litter tray, only instead of a bag of litter he had straw from the nearest farmyard. And although what he produced hardly smelled at all, Mrs Hansen cleaned up after him several times a day.

She also seemed to be devoting a good deal of time and attention to providing him with food. Not really knowing if Greg could understand her or not, she kept on talking at length about healthy organic diets: unsprayed, no artificial fertilisers, nothing genetically modified, providing everything the body needs and very rich in nutrients.

And really Greg couldn't complain: his vegetarian menus were lavish and varied. He wondered what the local farmers and greengrocers thought of the vast quantities of green stuff the Hansens were buying these days. At least he had something or other to nibble almost the whole day long. And there did seem to be some point in all this compulsive eating, because Greg felt sure he was still growing.

As for Ben, he left Greg in peace most of the time. He was usually out in the afternoon and evening. Sometimes he did things with Pa on the computer, the way he always used to. Sometimes you heard the sound of drums and bass from his room, booming through the house. Greg used to get fed up enough with that in the past, and now, thanks to his unusually keen sense of hearing, he was forced to coil up and pull his head in to get away from the noise.

I don't want to hear any more from outside, Greg thought, trying to reprogramme himself. I want to lead my own life all by myself!

For the moment, having been confined to his room for quite a while was a minor problem. I'll get out of here some time, thought Greg the caterpillar. He felt sure of it. First I'll wait and see exactly what Ma meant when she said, 'Make yourself comfortable in your own room for the time being, Greggy. We'll think of something, I know we will. You must just be patient!' Then Greg heard the familiar sound of the key turning in the keyhole, and he was locked in again.

What his father was doing was a mystery to Greg, as usual. He knew about Pa's stressful, time-consuming job. He'd hardly ever seen him when he wasn't either under pressure or absorbed in some activity. Looking at the computer with Ben. Discussing the technology of the future with Ben. Deep in building plans or discussions of money with Ma, or studying papers in the room next door.

He hardly ever came into Greg's room these days, simply appearing in the doorway now and then to reassure himself that everything was all right with the old fellow – or rather, the new fellow.

Only once were there problems – and then they were bad ones.

Greg had just gone under his bed, and was beginning to invent some new episodes for the stories about his two comic-strip characters. Even though it was all in his imagination, and he couldn't actually get the stories down on paper now, the thrill of thinking them up was the same as ever. And just at the most exciting moment he was disturbed. First by footsteps. Unmistakably Pa's. Then by the sound of the key. Not the way Ma turned it either. Then the noise of the door opening. Ever since it had been repaired it squealed horribly. And then there were a lot of footsteps marching around the room. They finally stopped beside the bed.

'Hey, come on out!'

Pa's voice sounded peculiar and uncertain of itself.

'Come on out! I brought you something to eat.'

Well, well . . . the first offer of food from the big boss himself!

'Come on, why are you hiding? I've got something to show you.'

Very odd. What was this strange note in Pa's voice in aid of?

Greg took his time. He wasn't going to do what he was told like a good, well-trained pet. But then his curiosity got the better of him. Activate the back pair of legs. Then the second pair from the back. Then . . .

Then a nasty shock. No sooner was Greg right out from under the bed than there was a click, a flash, and a buzz. And again. Click! Flash! Buzz!

'Good . . . great . . . that's got it!'

Greg felt both confused and dazzled. He stopped moving and tried to get his bearings.

Click! Flash! Buzz!

'There – and now from the side and the front . . .'

Click! Flash! Buzz . . . And something finally clicked inside Greg's head too. He's photographing me, he's actually taking photos without even asking me first!

It wasn't just anger or even rage, Greg also felt a very specific kind of discomfort, almost revulsion. Without stopping to think about it, he crawled up the nearest wall at high speed, faster than he'd ever thought he could go, and from there along the ceiling and down to the top of the door frame.

'Stop! Wait! What's the idea?'

Pa's voice was loud, harsh and penetrating. Almost as the same moment as Greg got out of the room, Mrs Hansen emerged from the bathroom.

'What's going on?'

'Nothing, nothing . . . here, come back this minute!'

Flight! Freedom! Those were the only thoughts in Greg's head. But he didn't go the simplest way, straight down to the ground floor and then to the front door: he crawled on over the landing ceiling, winding his way past radiant halogen lamps, getting caught on the sharp edges of picture frames, leaving broken glass on the floor behind him.

'Stay here, Gregor! Don't do anything silly – look, I didn't mean to startle you!'

'Greggy!' Mrs Hansen joined in, racing her husband downstairs.

By now Greg had been forced to a halt. Just as he might have expected, the front door was locked, and all other ways out of the house were closed. The Hansens had their reputation to think of, after all. Greg felt as he used to feel during earlier, two-legged escapades: they too had usually been brought to a sudden halt just before he reached a door, or soon after he was through it.

I'll be more cunning about it next time, Greg determined. He set off back of his own accord, up the stairs this time, and not quite so fast. Something or other hurt quite badly. Two things, in fact – one inside, one outside.

'Look, he's hurt himself! And what are you doing with that camera?' Greg heard his mother say before he disappeared into his room again.

Soon she was back with more herbal tinctures, fresh lettuce and words of comfort. But the caterpillar had coiled up again. For now, Greg didn't want to know.

It was the constant hunger that brought Greg back to the present. At the same time, he had another uncomfortable feeling, getting perceptibly stronger. It was a feeling deep down inside. Greg had experienced something like it before. It was connected with a sense of foreboding, and his suspicions were soon confirmed.

'Please don't be alarmed, Dr Schwarz! We're faced with a riddle ourselves. We daren't talk about it out loud.'

'We hesitated a long time. We were going to wait for this frightful thing to pass off. You're the first person we've taken into our confidence.'

'We need your help, we really do. Our ... our child ...'

Greg's heart began beating faster. It also began beating louder. He heard voices and footsteps coming closer. This was really exciting – like your birthday, Christmas, and end-of-term reports all on the same day.

'Please don't be alarmed. Er . . . what you see is likely to surprise you.'

The doctor was definitely annoyed now. 'Got a rash, has he? Had an epileptic fit? What do you suppose there is I haven't seen already in the course of my career? Two years in Accident and Emergency I've had, two years in Tropical Diseases, two years in an Aids hospice – '

'Doctor, we're not talking about ordinary medical phenomena of that nature. Something has happened here that – '

Greg had been listening to every word, but now he heard no more for quite a while. He lay in the middle of the room, with his favourite ball in front of him.

Silence. A long, long silence.

Greg didn't move.

'This is some kind of practical joke!'

And that was it.

First the doctor marched out of the room, then Pa, and finally Ma.

'Absolutely grotesque! I thought you'd called me out about something serious.'

The front door opening.

'Dr Schwarz, let me remind you that as a doctor it's your duty to keep silent – '

'I'd have thought it was my duty to report you for time-wasting. Absurd, absolutely absurd!'

The front door closing.

As a result of this scene, both Hansen parents flew off the handle. Mr Hansen had a fit of rage and needed a brandy in the middle of the day. Mrs Hansen burst into tears and needed a brandy too.

Greg was wide awake, registering everything.

Even rather enjoying it? He smiled secretly to himself. He'd been ignored often enough. People refused to take him seriously. But now he was a caterpillar, there was no overlooking him. All chaos might break loose any moment. And this was only the start of it – in the pit of his huge, hungry stomach Greg felt confident of that.

It wasn't till Ben put in an appearance that the atmosphere in the house changed.

Greg heard his brother comforting their mother, and then making her tell him all about it, down to the last detail. Ben's reaction was clear and straightforward, and he wouldn't listen to any objections.

'You just won't face facts. You want to hush it all up, gloss it over, and what do you get? Embarrassing scenes like that with the doctor! Okay, so this thing's happened, right? Greg's gone away, and his successor is sitting up there turning the place into a pigsty. It's no good asking me or yourselves or some antiquated old doctor *how* a thing like this can happen. There are specialists for these cases: zoologists, geneticists – oh, I don't know, futurologists or whatever! That's the way of the world. I mean, you two are still living in the last millennium and you daren't step into the next one. Those are the facts, and we have to do something!'

Greg had enjoyed every word of this. He might have problems of his own with his brother, but this speech impressed him.

It seemed to have taken effect on his parents too: that evening and all next day there was a great deal of telephoning, almost non-stop, behind closed doors. Ben was bunking off school. He had obviously joined the family council, and later he spent hours doing research on the Internet with Pa.

Greg, on the other hand, wanted no part in any of this. He knew what *he* thought, and there was something he wished for so badly that he thought up a plan, a plan that wouldn't go out of his head.

Sara.

* * *

The next thing to happen wasn't planned either – but to Greg it was manna from heaven.

This time it wasn't Grandfather's bed standing outside the front door, but a taxi. The driver hooted like mad and wouldn't take no for an answer: his fare was demanding to be let into the house, and he would see to the baggage himself.

Soon after that Mr Brandenburg, Greg's grandfather, was there in person – looking rather frail, but with some sarcasm in his voice when he spoke.

'Don't worry, I don't plan to be a burden on you for long. But say what you like, I'm taking you up on your offer of a room here – and I'm sure I can manage to avoid this special virus of Greg's.'

There was no more to be said. After all, his room had been ready for ages, and after a few hours everyone realised there was no way to keep Grandfather away from the mutated Greg. The Hansens had certainly fixed it so that Grandfather could live entirely on the ground floor, because he had difficulty with walking – but as soon as the old gentleman had settled into his room he climbed upstairs secretly, in some pain, to visit the sick, namely his favourite grandson.

Knock, knock at the door. No answer.

Knock, knock in Greg's heart. He knew who was there.

'Why in the world are they shutting the boy up?'

Mr Brandenburg was not usually given to talking to himself, but he had realised ever since arriving that there was something odd going on in this house, and he had to discuss it with someone.

'Father?' called Mrs Hansen from downstairs. She thought she'd heard noises.

'Paul?' Mr Hansen was concerned too.

Creak, click ... Mr Brandenburg entered Greg's room.

'Grandfather?' Ben emerged from his room.

'Greg? *Greg*?'

By now the Hansen family, or that part of it that went around on two legs, had gathered in Greg's room.

'Why isn't the lad in his bed?'

'Probably *under* his bed right now,' said Ben.

'How very interesting.' Grandfather bent down, groaning slightly. 'Greg? I'm visiting the sick. Thought I'd bring you a couple of wildlife videos.'

'Paul, please! Can we speak to you alone for a moment? Outside, not here where . . .'

The old man might be visibly weaker than before, and he wasn't entirely able to hide his present state of confusion, but his voice was firm and decided.

'You surprise me, children, you really do! I always thought you took your old father seriously. I didn't think you believed I was a fool. Kindly let me talk to Ben alone.'

Although Mr and Mrs Hansen couldn't remember when they had last been thrown out of a room like that, they obeyed, and Grandfather closed the door behind them.

'Now then, boy,' he said to Ben. 'Let's have the truth. The whole truth, please.'

Ben thought for a moment. A smile flitted across his face. He cast an enquiring glance at the bed, and then started on the explanations.

'Well, Greg isn't Greg any more, see?'

'How interesting.'

'It's kind of a mutation, know what I mean? Some mega-futuristic whatsit's turned our Greg into something else.'

'How interesting.'

'You wouldn't believe the things that have been going on in this house, Grandfather. We don't any of us know what to make of it.'

'And where have you hidden this mutation of Greg, if I may ask?'

'Er ... well, he sometimes hides of his own accord, under the bed there.'

'Thank you, Ben. Would you leave us alone now, please?'

'But honest, it's true, Grandfather.'

'I appreciate that, Ben.'

Things are hotting up, thought Greg. Now I'll have to come out of hiding, and Grandfather will get the shock of his life.

Ben had left the room. Grandfather's warm, wonderfully sympathetic voice said, again, 'Greg?'

Come on, be brave! Nothing can happen to you, Greg! He'll soon get over it . . .

Greg twitched a couple of times. He was feeling short of space. Recently, he'd hardly been able to squeeze under the bed. He put out his feelers, and his decision to come out into the open set him moving from down at his far end.

Calm. A tense sort of calm, but calm.

Greg could smell his grandfather, and now, for the first time since changing shape, he was really sorry he couldn't see clearly any more.

He was excited, but he felt no fear. He crawled out of hiding until he was revealed at full length. Then he didn't know what to do next. Should he just lie there in front of Grandfather? Or climb up on the bed? Or crawl up the walls?

'Is that you, Greg?'

Good question. Greg couldn't answer it himself. But for the first time in a long while – to him, it seemed an eternity – he tried to make some kind of noise other than biting and munching.

'Yyy . . . mmm . . .'

For a split second it seemed as if he might manage more than this pathetic sound. The words were all there in his head . . . plenty of words, plenty of sentences. But at the same time, Greg felt there was no real need to answer in words.

Who or what is Greg anyway? Just a name? Something more? A human being yesterday, a caterpillar today. And what tomorrow?

'Well, you're certainly very handsome.'

Those words made him feel good. Amazingly good. Greg just lay there, basking in the presence of someone he felt he didn't know nearly well enough, although he'd always been fond of Grandfather. Without saying so, usually, and now he *couldn't* say so.

'Isn't this something of a prison for you? I mean, won't a person like you die kept in confinement?'

A sense of excitement arose in Greg, but he kept still. Out of his multifaceted eyes, he saw the large, long shape that was Grandfather moving away from him towards the window.

'Paul?' called Mr Hansen, from downstairs.

'I feel sure you need fresh air and exercise.'

'Father?'

The window was opened. Cool night air wafted into the room. Greg felt an urge to get moving.

'Go on, then, enjoy your freedom! I'll leave the window open, so you can get back in any time you like.'

The old man stepped aside and went to the door. Greg felt an overwhelming urge to get outside as quickly as he could! Down the outside wall and away from the house!

After that, Greg the caterpillar knew every inch of the way, every obstacle he'd encounter – he had been through it in his imagination over and over again these last few days.

'Paul, aren't you feeling well?'

'Oh, Father, why did you have to come up here? Honestly, you take such whims into your head!'

'Don't worry, Helen. Better whimsical than weak-minded. I was only letting your delightful pet out in the fresh air.'

'Letting him . . . ?'

'You did *what*?'

Greg would have enjoyed listening to the rest of this, but he had to watch every step he took: he was going out into the dark, and what he left behind him was less exciting than what lay ahead.

It was a difficult journey. His many legs weren't used to the difference between soft grass and sharp-edged gravel, to crossing rough wooden planks, flower-beds and smooth asphalt, and then crawling through a field of oilseed rape that seemed to go on for ever. And then there was the excited feeling. No Greg, no caterpillar could just ignore it. Somewhere, far away but too near for comfort, there was a search party with torches and car headlights, but luckily it was sticking close to the Hansens' house.

All was quiet and dark in front of Greg's feelers. Well, almost dark. On the far side of the field he saw a light, and he had no trouble at all in locating it. He'd been watching that spot for weeks, from the Hansens' kitchen window or garden terrace. The lighted window usually went dark around eleven at night, later at weekends. Greg couldn't say when it would go dark tonight; he had lost all sense of time, and didn't know the day of the week or the time of day. He just knew what he wanted – even if the whole idea was totally crazy. Also dangerous.

How would she react if she saw him? Wouldn't he give her a terrible shock? Would she start screaming, or run for her parents?

These and other confused thoughts were churning

around in Greg's mind as he made straight for the Austers' house under cover of darkness.

And then he'd made it. He was lying right under Sara's lighted window, in the middle of a flower-bed. He couldn't be bothered about the flower-bed right now. Above him was the light in the window, and rhythmical music, the kind of music he liked. Darkness along one side of the house, light flooding out of an open French window on the other. There were sounds from there too: music that Greg didn't like so much, voices he couldn't make out.

So now what? Up to this point he had been acting as if he were on automatic pilot. Now Greg had his doubts.

How was Sara to know who he was? Maybe she was scared of large animals. Had Ben perhaps mentioned some horrible monster shaped like a caterpillar?

Well, I have to try! At least I must find out where she is at this moment.

Heart thudding worse than ever, Greg the caterpillar made his way, step by tiny step, up to the window-sill.

Now to raise his head, and then . . .

'Grrr!'

Greg froze in his tracks.

Alarm. Anxiety. Rage.

That dog! Of course! How come he'd forgotten that silly yapping little thing, the dog the Austers had idiotically taken on board as a pet?

'Grrr! Grrr!'

Now what? Where did he go from here?

Just as Greg had decided to try climbing further up, a light went on on the first floor, and next moment a veranda door opened and a female voice called, 'Dogmatix?'

'Yap-yap . . . grrr!'

It was pure instinct rather than deliberate thought that set Greg moving: he climbed straight down, right towards the little dog.

'Grrr!' This time it didn't sound quite so fierce, but the dog wasn't moving from the spot.

'Is there anyone there?'

Greg had reached the flower-bed.

'Sara, switch the outside lights on!'

Greg saw the little animal, smelled its dogginess, and its fear, and could think of nothing but escape. But just at that moment, the light went on, and just at that moment little Dogmatix obviously decided to show what a brave dog he was. He jumped at Greg from behind – the spiky red thing obviously fascinated him. From biology lessons at school, Greg dimly remembered that on caterpillars it was called a cornicle. The dog howled, then there was a penetrating smell that Greg himself found unpleasant, and he supposed his stinging hairs had worked as well, because his opponent had disappeared.

Everything else went smoothly. Greg tried to get away from the light as fast as he could. It seemed to be searching for him from several sources at once.

'Wait – look, what's that?'

'I don't believe it!'

'Careful, it's gigantic! You stay here!'

Greg followed his own scent back as fast as he could. Just keep going straight ahead home, he thought. For a while, he sensed the pursuit, and then it faded away. With the last of his strength, Greg clambered up over the fence, through the garden, and up to his own room. The window was open, the halogen lamp by the bed was on, as usual – but somehow he couldn't crawl under the bed any more . . .

Greg coiled up on the floor just where he was and drew his head in. Exhausted as he was, he felt that unpleasant twitching again, but he had no energy left to bother about it. He fell fast asleep.

Three

When Greg woke up again he felt dreadful.

Was he hungry?

He could smell several different varieties of fresh lettuce right beside him – but he didn't feel like eating just now. Instead, he had this strange new feeling, a feeling he couldn't control any more than he could control his constant twitchings.

'There, Greggy, see what I've brought you!'

Ma's voice was kind and gentle as usual, but Greg still wasn't interested. In fact, her eternal 'Greggy' was getting on his nerves. Badly.

'What's the matter? Can we do anything to help?'

I can manage by myself, thanks, Greg would have liked to say, although he wasn't really sure of it any more.

Further away, he heard voices: one was his father's – agitated, uncertain of itself, and much too loud. The other was female, rather shy, much softer.

'Greggy, can you hear me?'

Mrs Hansen was kneeling in front of the coiled-up caterpillar, making tender stroking movements just above his back without actually touching him. Her face showed the traces of several sleepless nights.

'We just don't know what to do, Greggy! We've called someone in to examine you.'

No! Greg felt a great dislike of this idea, though he had no way of expressing it. He'd already coiled up. He had pulled his head in too. And he'd already tried out his few other ways of defending himself – they might scare a small dog, or annoy Ben, but that was about it.

'Please go carefully examining him, Dr Rossetti! He may be asleep. Take a look for yourself!'

Pa's voice was the last thing Greg heard before he fell into a kind of fit. Twitching and jerking, he pushed his way along the floor. He felt an irresistible urge to stretch and stretch . . . he was nothing but body . . . for an eternity he was nothing but this caterpillar body with all its segments and all its feet . . .

Then, at last, things calmed down. A sense of well-being spread through his whole giant body. Waking up was like stepping into a new world. Or rather, a new Greg stepping into the old world. That was more like it.

'He never did anything like that before!' whispered Mr Hansen.

'He looks quite different now!' said Mrs Hansen, equally softly.

'It's shed its skin, that's all,' said the strange woman's voice.

Sara's fault . . . all Sara's fault. This thought went through Greg's mind, but he couldn't make any more of it.

'Yes, you . . . you certainly described the creature accurately. That is very definitely a caterpillar. Where – er, where did you get it from?'

Before anyone could answer, the mobile phone in Mr Hansen's jacket pocket rang.

'Yes . . . yes, Hansen Architectural Bureau – Thomas Hansen here.'

From a distance, Greg heard a voice he had heard only once before, and very recently too: a man's voice, extremely upset and agitated.

'Please, Mr Auster, I can explain!'

Greg caught the sound of another flood of words. Then his father spoke again.

'Yes, Mr Auster, yes, I know you're a solicitor. No, it's a perfectly harmless creature. It's usually kept shut up. There was an accident . . .'

'Tell him we'll look in and see him. After all, the

children know each other,' Mrs Hansen put in.

'Mr Auster, we're as keen to be on good terms with our neighbours as you are. The fact is, my wife and I have had a lot to cope with recently. And surely reporting this incident to the police would do nobody any . . .'

Greg listened, still noticing that he felt very well: the twitching had stopped, his whole body felt relaxed and sort of liberated. Also, he could feel that he had grown visibly. Then, out of nowhere, his old urge to eat came back – uninhibited, uncontrollable. Greg stretched his head right out and made for the green stuff. The conversation no longer interested him as he started greedily on the lettuce leaves.

Unknown species . . . never encountered one before . . . very much doubt if it features in the scientific books . . . probably of sub-tropical origin . . . however, while typical of the genus, also quite extraordinary . . . keep the old skin carefully . . . yes, the new skin is often lighter and brighter in colour . . . would certainly be a great attraction in the zoo . . . colleague of mine who works in a research institute . . . would be extremely interested . . .

A few scraps of the conversation had penetrated Greg's mind after all. At some point they had all left his room, and even downstairs they seemed to be talking in whispers. The loudest thing Greg could hear was the birds twittering in the garden. During a short break in his meal, he noticed that, as he had feared, his window was firmly locked again.

Why he felt better than ever in this new caterpillar outfit was a mystery to Greg. The failure of his expedition into the outside world still weighed on his mind, in so far as there was room in his mind for thoughts of anything but lettuce. At the same time Greg could guess what was coming, and he began planning for it. He felt more adventurous than ever before – as a caterpillar, as Greg Hansen, as a living creature of any kind, full stop. And he had this sense that his peaceful domestic existence was about to come to an end. A premonition. By now he knew he could rely on his premonitions.

He was living in interesting times. Ben confirmed it when he came to pay Greg a visit, bringing fresh vegetables in, and something else too – something that smelled very much like jelly babies.

'Hey, what came over *you*, then? The neighbours were in a blue funk! And you had to go and do it round at the Austers', of all places!'

Carry on, Greg felt like saying, I don't mind! He was surprised to realise that for the first time he genuinely didn't mind about his brother.

Plop!

How that little accident came to happen at this precise moment he wasn't at all sure. Still, he said to himself, who cares?

'Oh, charming! Nice life you've picked for yourself, I must say. Okay, little one, look what I've brought you!'

Ben held a packet of jelly babies open in front of Greg's jaws. He longed to get at them.

'The acid test! If you like these, then you really are my brother. If you don't, I agree that you ought to be in the zoo.'

Zoo?

Greg immediately raised his front segments up in the air. It looked almost as if he wanted to talk to Ben.

'That's right, the zoo! Hey . . . I think you just understood what I said!'

The zoo? They couldn't be serious! Greg stayed where he was, waiting for Ben to go on.

'Or the circus, if I can teach you a few tricks! Come on, little extra-terrestrial brother! A bit higher up now – beg nicely, and you can have three jelly babies. Go on, then, beg nicely!'

The so-and-so! Greg felt his little red cornicle moving, and all his protective hairs bristled. He wanted to go for Ben, although Ben was much larger and stronger and would have the advantage over him.

'What is it, little mutated brotherkins?'

Fart!

It was loud and clear, and Greg just couldn't restrain himself. Even Ben seemed taken aback by this new way of communicating.

'That wasn't very polite, was it?'

Greg's answer was to do what he'd been wanting to do all this time – he lunged at Ben's hand, grabbed the bag of jelly babies in his jaws, and started munching.

'Are you off your head, little monster?'

At that moment the door was flung open, and an agitated Mr Hansen came in. 'Ben, you must go over and see those Austers at once! Talk to the girl, or the mother. That sh – that solicitor, Auster, I mean – he's obviously been on to the press. I've had three reporters ringing in a row, wanting to know where we live, asking for interviews. Get the Austers over here, or try to fix a time we can all meet. I've already tried ringing his office to discuss it privately, but our solicitor friend's permanently in a meeting, or so they say!'

Fart!

There it was again.

'Should have brought him up better,' Ben pointed out.

'You can leave out the wisecracks! I warn you, I'm going to pieces.'

And the door slammed.

What a happy household, thought Greg, getting down to the rest of the jelly babies.

Downstairs the ordinary phone and the mobile phone were both ringing frantically. In between, the fax squeaked. At one point Mrs Hansen uttered a loud screech, and the front door was closed with a bang. Grandfather could clearly be heard complaining of all this racket in a house in a quiet part of the country.

As for the caterpillar, in so far as caterpillars can be amused, he was having a very amusing time.

It wasn't until that evening that Greg had another visitor, one he'd been expecting: Grandfather Paul knocked, then came into the room and closed the door behind him.

Greg happened to be on his way across the ceiling, taking a constitutional for the sake of his digestion. For a moment he wasn't sure what to do.

'You can stay up there if you like. I don't object to people looking down on me.'

That voice – that special voice of his, thought Greg. He wanted to be as close to Grandfather as possible.

'Well, that's life . . .'

Grandfather sat down on the bed, with some difficulty, and Greg lay at his feet, partly coiled up. Suddenly he felt he'd been in exactly the same situation before, ages ago – he and Grandfather, sitting just like this, and in the same mood. But surely he hadn't been a caterpillar then?

'Yes, that's life. Both simple and complicated. Simply complicated. Complicated in a simple kind of way.'

Greg listened, drinking in every word Grandfather uttered in his deep voice.

'A person plans to spend the evening of his life peacefully in the country with his children and grand-children, and what happens? Strange, very strange . . .'

Greg, still listening to every word, felt cross when he heard Ben coming upstairs.

'Sometimes I think I must be at the movies, watching a science-fiction film or something similar. In my old age I feel very close to the future. But then I remember none of this is really anything new. There've been amazing creatures like you on earth for ever. It's only in the last couple of hundred years that life has got rather boring. All the same, something does bother me . . .'

Grandfather stopped, and Greg felt uneasy. Ben was standing there, right outside the door of his room, listening.

'I don't know if you can understand everything I say, but I want to tell you a story anyway.'

At this point Greg could no longer keep still.

'Oh, I don't mind Ben listening,' said Grandfather, as if he could read Greg's thoughts. 'Come on in, Ben!'

Greg was rather annoyed.

'Sorry, didn't want to disturb you,' said Ben, 'but Ma says I'm to tell you, whatever you do don't open that window.'

'I'll think about it, Ben, I'll think about it. Sit down, why don't you? You might be interested in my story too.'

The old man paused for some time before he went on.

'Almost a hundred years ago, an author called Kafka wrote a story about a young man who wakes up one morning to find he's turned into a giant beetle. It may be just coincidence, but that young man's name was Gregor too. He lived with his parents, and you can imagine what a shock it was to them all. No one knew what to make of his sudden metamorphosis. No one understood the poor fellow, and he couldn't defend himself. In the end he perished miserably, there in his room.'

Grandfather stopped. Greg felt rather unwell.

'But that's only a story,' said Ben. 'I mean, this is

real. That thing there is genuine. So we've got real problems with it.'

'Everything becomes a story at some point,' said Grandfather, rising with some difficulty. 'I only wanted to tell you that one to make sure this new story of ours doesn't end tragically too.'

'So what *is* going to happen? What can we do? What do you suggest, Grandfather?'

'People always say the old shouldn't interfere with the young. And there's sure to be something in what people always say.'

'All the same, we have to keep the doors and windows closed,' said Ben. 'I mean, some of our neighbours don't like creatures like this around the place.'

Greg felt he couldn't stand this any more. He wanted to follow Ben out to the top of the stairs and do something unpleasant to him, but Grandfather barred the way.

'Listen, caterpillar,' he said quietly, and Greg felt him looming overhead like a large and friendly shadow. 'Let me give you a piece of advice: go your way, your own personal way, and don't let anyone stop you! Remember that!'

Greg had been planning to think hard about the story

his grandfather had just told, but instead he felt ravenously hungry again.

And there was something else: Greg didn't feel happy in his room any more. It wasn't just that it felt too small and cramped for him. He suddenly felt he wanted to demolish everything, or almost everything, that was part of the old days. He wanted to destroy the whole lot of it.

Doing the best his jaws would allow, he began tearing down the football posters from the walls, shredding his brightly coloured bedclothes, nibbling his old books, in fact attacking everything that reminded him of his former life.

Mrs Hansen came into the room in the middle of this operation.

'For goodness' sake! Stop it!'

This exclamation usually did make Greg stop whatever he was doing. But today all his many feet were itching, and the itch was also particularly strong in his jaws: first, get the Bravo poster down off the wall, now for the school timetable up beside his desk . . . For the time being Greg felt satisfied.

'What on earth is the matter with you?'

Mrs Hansen had been watching helplessly as he rampaged around the room. Although she kept trying to suppress the thought, she did begin to doubt whether this creature before her could really still be Greg.

'Oh, please listen to me. I'm at my wits' end.'

Greg was enjoying the situation. At last he'd summoned up the courage to let rip! At last everything was revolving around *him*, not around the stress of Ma's alternative medicine course, or Pa's architectural problems, or Ben's latest adventures on the Internet.

'And please don't run off like that again! We're doing all we can to make you feel comfortable, hoping things will turn out all right in the end. But you've put us in such an awkward position. We have to keep telling lies the whole time!'

No, you don't, Greg wanted to say.

'We have to tell lies to your school, to our friends, to all the family except for Paul. Thomas doesn't have the time to keep his clients happy. Ben's neglecting his lessons. And I can't seem to memorise a single medical term for the exam, not to mention the seminars I've missed and my weekend work groups. And then there's the anxiety – what if it all comes out?'

In some surprise, Greg realised that just now these considerations left him almost entirely cold. He had that empty feeling inside his stomach again. He was glad when this time, surprisingly, his father came into the room with some green stuff.

'Here – something nice for our new household pet!'

This was probably meant to be hilariously funny. To Greg's surprise, his father squatted down right on the floor and waved a fresh lettuce leaf in front of him.

'Fresh from the farm – biodynamic and unsprayed!'

He's lying! He's trying to trick me. Greg felt sure of it. He also thought he could sense his parents exchanging silent signals.

'Look, your very favourite kind of lettuce!'

Oh, get stuffed! thought Greg. I'll show him how. And he started on the lettuce. His jaws crunched and scrunched. His whole being was intent on filling his stomach.

A few minutes later, Greg was unconscious. He lay there as if asleep, his head partly drawn in and over to one side. His feelers and the hairs along his sides drooped limply. His alarming mock face with the camouflage markings had folded in, and the threatening red colour had drained away from the cornicle at his far end.

'Please handle him very carefully. We don't know which are the most sensitive bits of him.'

Two uniformed ambulance men came into Greg's room carrying a stretcher. They stared blankly at the creature in front of them.

'Good heavens – is it real?' asked one of them.

'What did you use to anaesthetise it?' asked the other.

'Liquid carbon dioxide gas, and no more questions, please!' said Mr Hansen. He had patches of red on his face. 'I'm paying you huge sums to do your job and keep your mouths shut, all right?'

'Well, sorry, but never in our whole professional lives – this is certainly a first for us!'

'It's a first for us too,' said Mrs Hansen. She was paler than she'd looked since the day Greg was born. 'Please go *very* gently. He's extremely sensitive!'

Soon afterwards the caterpillar Greg was strapped to the stretcher, entirely covered by a white sheet. Even Ben kept his mouth shut until they'd all reached the front door. Then he said, 'Careful – there's some of those characters hanging around outside again!'

'Not a word to anyone! And close the door behind us at once!' said Mr Hansen. 'The answerphone's switched on. I'll get in touch on my mobile as soon as I know any more.'

Ben's warning was a timely one. No sooner had Mr Hansen and the two men left the house, making for the ambulance, than several journalists armed with cameras rushed towards their prey.

'Can you tell us if the victim is a family member?'

'Is there any truth in the rumours that you're

keeping imported exotic animals in this house?'

'Are you really just an architect, or do you breed these exotic species yourself?'

'Oh, get out!' shouted Mr Hansen.

The rest of the operation was conducted in silence. The stretcher was pushed into the ambulance. Mr Hansen and one of the ambulance men got in beside it. The other man climbed into the driver's seat, closed the door, and drove Greg away with the light on top of the ambulance flashing.

The first thing Greg became aware of, after quite some time, was conveyed through his sense of smell, and was confusing.

Deep down in Greg's subconscious, there was already an extraordinary mixture of many odours churning about. Camel and lion dung. Monkey pee. Bear droppings. Llama saliva and horse dung. And, and, and . . .

It wasn't until a little later that he could hear, too – nothing like as clearly as usual, and it was almost impossible to tell one voice from another. It was like listening to them through a huge wad of cotton wool.

'Almost certainly of the male sex . . . astonishing conformity to all the typical features of the genus . . . no sign whatsoever of any human structures . . . short life expectancy may certainly be assumed ... scientific research reduced *ad absurdum* in every way ... care in the zoological department out of the question ... our sympathy and genuine concern ... of course, yes, discretion of the very essence ...'

Slowly, very slowly, Greg recovered full consciousness. His sense of sight, nothing to write home about anyway, still wasn't working too well, but he could tell that his father was somewhere around. In fact, he could sense Pa's anxiety and embarrassment. As if he had some thawing out to do, he found he could move his legs and get the segments of his body loosened up only with unusual difficulty.

'Well, as we've already said, Mr Hansen, here's what we can offer you: there's a very progressive Institute of Genetics based locally, equipped to apply the latest laboratory techniques. And we are sure that its director, Dr Markstein – that's Professor Markstein – will make an appointment to see you and your pet at once.'

'Couldn't you get him to come here?' asked Mr Hansen.

What's going on? What are they going to do to me? All of a sudden Greg felt wide awake. He raised his head, and then his front segments, and somehow he felt as if he were even using his blind eyes, the camouflage markings intended to scare people.

'Careful!'

'Watch out!'

'Keep calm,' said Pa's voice. It sounded unusually strange and unsure of itself.

'Sure you've got a good grip on it?'

'Yes, of course.'

All this was more of an irritant to Greg than anything – every smell, every word, and the dark shadows surrounding him; they were all irritants. He crawled frantically away, looking for the nearest way to climb up. He had to get out of this confined space!

'Watch out – the apparatus!'

Something fell over with a crash. Glass broke on the floor.

'Do something! Stop it!'

'Greg, come on down! No one's going to hurt you!'

Hungry. I'm hungry! The anaesthetic had suppressed that instinct for a while, but now it surfaced again, demandingly, and at the same time Greg felt very weak. As weak as he used to feel after running a thousand metres.

'Come on, here, we've got just what you'd like to eat!'

Well, someone around here seemed to know how to treat a caterpillar. Doors were opened and closed again. The smell of green leaves made its way to Greg. It was obvious that he was in a trap. But oddly enough, it was the thought of Sara that induced Greg to give in and start eating for all he was worth.

Four

The drive back showed Greg that a new chapter of his life had now begun.

Once he had taken the edge off his hunger, he lay down of his own accord on the stretcher, and let them strap him down without resisting. He wasn't sorry to say goodbye to all those hundreds of different animal smells, either.

As soon as the door was closed, however, and the ambulance had started, all hell broke loose.

'We're being followed!' Greg heard the driver say over the intercom.

'Drive faster! Switch the siren and the blue light on!'

'No, don't do anything to make us conspicuous!' Greg's father put in.

'Oh, hell – it's the same as on the way here. I thought that was just chance.'

'What kind of car is it following?' asked Mr Hansen.

'I'll call the control centre, get them to tell the police.'

'No, not the police – keep this under wraps!' cried Mr Hansen.

As the conversation got more and more frantic, so did the drive. The tyres underneath Greg were squealing almost constantly. There was hooting outside, and the sound of vehicles braking, and then, from somewhere, the howl of a second siren, and then a third.

Listening to the chaos, Greg didn't know which was giving his stomach more trouble: lack of food, or all this chasing around bends.

His arrival home was no less eventful than the drive. Two police patrol cars drew up at the same time as the ambulance, and several cars and two motorbikes were parked a little way further off, on the field track which usually saw no traffic except the occasional tractor or combine harvester.

'Don't talk to anyone! Don't say anything!' Mr Hansen was trying to keep the situation under control. 'You'll be okay,' he added, speaking to Greg in paternal tones as he carefully spread the white cloth over him.

This is the last time I let anyone treat me like that, Greg decided. It was quite fun to have all this going on around him, but he really hated being strapped down. What was more, the whole operation was only now becoming clear to him – thinking backwards, and skipping over a large blank in his memory, he conjured up the scene when Pa fed him that lettuce.

'Fresh from the farm – unsprayed!'

And Ma knew exactly what was going on . . . How mean of them, pretending to be nice and kind and fooling him like that!

The Hansens negotiated with the police in private, where Greg couldn't hear them. No stranger was allowed to catch a glimpse of him as he was taken back to his room and let loose there.

What a relief! Now he could relax. Alone at last!

First of all he went sniffing around the place. Along the floor. Over all four walls and the ceiling. In the process, Greg, rather bewildered, registered: Something's different around here. Ma must have finished the clearing-up job I started. Then he felt that uncontrollable hunger again. If I don't eat I won't grow, he thought. And if I don't grow, then nothing in my life will change. It's as simple as that, said Greg to himself in a matter-of-fact sort of way, and he crawled over to his feeding place, where he found plenty of provisions.

He sniffed suspiciously at the green stuff, but his

jaws practically had a life of their own. They tucked in greedily. Lettuce first. Then dandelion leaves. Then some new but very tasty kind of vegetable ... Caterpillars don't usually eat so many different things, Greg remembered from one of his wildlife videos.

What do you mean, caterpillar? Greg asked himself.

What do you mean, Greg? the caterpillar asked him back.

Soon afterwards, Greg heard footsteps. It was his mother coming upstairs. He hadn't eaten nearly enough to satisfy his hunger, but Greg dropped the leaf he had been nibbling, drew his head in and coiled up.

Mrs Hansen opened the door.

'Greggy?'

Greg pretended not to hear.

'Am I disturbing you, Greggy?'

Greg was relishing the situation. I'll let her know I'm cross with her! She helped to trick me with that drugged lettuce. She's part of the conspiracy to keep me shut up in here.

'Do you feel happier with your room now? It's so hard to know what you really want.'

Oh no, here we go again, thought Greg soberly. There's something in her voice I don't seem able to resist. I can never be angry with her for long, even though she's almost as bad as the others about taking me seriously.

Then he had an idea. I'll test her, he thought.

As if he were just waking from a deep sleep, he slowly uncoiled and let his head emerge. Then he turned his whole body with an almost elegant movement – he found he was enjoying this kind of thing more and more – and crawled straight over to his mother on all fourteen feet.

Then he belched.

Well, never mind, all part of life's rich tapestry, said Greg to himself, refusing to feel embarrassed.

He stopped close to his mother, concentrated, and sent all his thoughts her way. Then he tried transmitting his own wishes.

I don't want to be shut up in here. I want to move about freely!

There was deathly silence in the room. Greg didn't move. His mother didn't move either.

Do you understand? Greg repeated his message again. I want to move about freely!

Sara reacted to my thoughts, he thought suddenly. Sara turned to look at me several times after I'd been thinking them.

'Is there something you want?' Mrs Hansen's question brought Greg back to his present caterpillar existence.

I – want – to – move – about – freely! said Greg, without making a sound.

'Do you want to move about the house freely? Would you feel better then?'

All of a sudden, Greg felt enormously happy. He couldn't help himself; he moved towards his mother, and rubbed his whole body against her legs. He hesitated for a moment, and realised he *was* feeling embarrassed this time.

Food! I must start eating again!

Greg set to work on the green stuff. But all the time he noticed the way his mother was sitting on the bed, motionless, looking and looking and looking at him.

Much later, Mr Hansen paid a visit to Greg too. He looked worn out. His face showed the signs of sleeplessness and all the agitation of the last few days.

Greg was just trying out some new movements of his body. He was pleased to find that he could stand on his three pairs of front legs and rear all his back segments up in the air at the same time.

This is great! thought Greg, deciding to take no notice of his father.

'Er . . .' began Pa, in an unusually quiet voice.

Greg noticed something moving at his back end.

'Er, I don't know if you can hear me . . .'

Plop.

'You see, it's a rather peculiar lifestyle of yours in

here, and I do have certain problems with it . . .'

Another plop! That was surprising.

'But I want to say I'm sorry about that drugged lettuce.'

I could always try a third plop, thought Greg, attempting to move forward on his front six legs.

'Look, I'm going to leave the door open.'

Greg was interested to hear that.

'Just one thing: please, please don't show yourself at the windows.'

Greg listened to his father's retreating footsteps. He was going into the bedroom, but that didn't interest Greg just now. He needed a nap himself to get fit for the night's exercise.

It was after midnight when Greg woke up again. The halogen lamp was burning, same as usual. Nothing stirred in the house. There was only a slight draught blowing over the floor of his room. They'd left the door open.

Greg set out. He had no particular aim in mind. He just wanted to enjoy the feeling of being able to crawl through almost all the rooms undisturbed. His nocturnal excursions of the past – first in their old flat, now in this house – seemed decades ago. So was the guilty conscience he'd always had about them. Tonight he was planning to be all caterpillar. With no memory. With no future. Just a caterpillar here and now in this house, which was so full of things to smell, feel and taste. It looked as if they'd left a few lights on specially for him and all his feet. The only thing denied to Greg was the view he longed for – or at least the idea of a view – because the roller shutters were down over every window in the house.

Hungry. He was hungry again. Of course.

Just as Greg was making for the larder and its stores of food, he heard voices. One of them familiar and babbling. Several not familiar, some of them babbling too, some of them stone cold sober. Shortly afterwards the front door was opened from outside, and Ben Hansen, not entirely sober himself, staggered into the hall.

'Nope . . . no interviews, no photos, our millennial monster's pupated, flown away . . . you'd need a chopper to catch up with my extra-terrestrial little brother . . . No, honest, no monster caterpillar sensational headlines . . . the crazy caterpillar gig's somewhere else!'

Click. The door closed. The reporters were outside. Ben was inside. Greg thought the whole thing was hilariously funny.

'You'd think everything revolved around our monster!' Ben muttered to himself. At that moment Greg appeared behind him.

'Hey, leave that out, creepy-crawly! You made me jump!'

Greg's back end was simply itching, but this time nothing came out – instead, it went up in the air, doing the trick he'd been practising a couple of hours earlier.

'That's a great trick, creepy-crawly! Going to join the circus after all?'

Greg answered in his own way: he started moving forward on his front six legs, making straight for his brother.

'Hey, don't look at me like that! I'm your brother! Your big brother, remember?'

Fart!

Belch! Ben had problems of his own . . .

'Am I going off my head, or what? Come on, I'm going to the kitchen. Need a drink. Get you a drink too?'

Greg was enjoying this. It was the first time Ben had ever made him such a generous offer. And although caterpillars don't get thirsty, he followed Ben – on all fourteen legs this time.

There wasn't much left to go wrong, but no sooner had Ben opened a bottle of beer, taken a hefty gulp from it himself, and started trying to give Greg some, staggering slightly the whole time, than Pa appeared in the doorway in his pyjamas.

'Ben!'

Greg felt his brother's alarm.

'Leave that caterpillar alone!'

'Just testing . . .'

What happened next was fast and ruthless: for once, Mr Hansen's attitude to his elder son was not as tolerant as usual. With some difficulty, he steered Ben upstairs and into his room. Then, taking no further notice of Greg, he disappeared into the parental bedroom.

Next morning the Hansen family ate breakfast on their feet, and directly after breakfast they held a council of war.

'The house is surrounded,' said Mr Hansen. 'We don't stand a chance.'

'We ought to go on the offensive. I thought so all along,' Ben joined in. He had sobered up by now.

'My nerves won't stand this. I don't feel capable of making any decisions,' said Mrs Hansen.

'Don't anyone take any notice of me – I'll be fine,' said Grandfather Paul, going back to his own room.

But he isn't really fine, he's feeling very ill, and nobody can help him – those were the ideas Greg picked up as he nibbled the lettuce leaves Mrs Hansen had put down for him in a big bowl near the fridge.

Mr Hansen's mobile phone rang for the umpteenth time. This time he answered it. 'Yes?'

'Am I speaking to Mr Thomas Hansen?'

'You are.'

'Glad to hear it. I've tried often enough. The Zoological Institute gave me your number. I'd like to offer you my assistance. My name is Dr Markstein, M-A-R-K-S-T-E-I-N, and I'm director of the Institute of Genetics . . .'

Greg would have liked to hear the rest of this conversation, but his father left the kitchen with the mobile phone, and the voice, which had an odd sound about it, died away in the distance.

Then the doorbell rang.

'Let's not answer it,' said Mrs Hansen.

'Why not?' asked Ben. 'Personally I'm in favour of letting the whole lot in at once, and then they'll leave us in peace. I mean, this new pet of ours isn't so very special. *I* got used to him ages ago. Sound effects and all.'

The bell rang more vigorously.

'Go and get your father. He can deal with it!'

Pretending to take no notice, Greg munched away. Something was about to happen. His seventh sense, or maybe it was his eighth, told him so.

The bell was ringing quite violently now, and Mr Hansen realised he would have to answer.

'We're not at home to visitors, we're not buying anything, we don't have anything to give away, kindly respect our privacy!'

Mr Hansen had spoken through the little peephole in the door, but the two men standing outside in grey overalls, carrying toolboxes, were not deterred.

'Sorry to disturb you, sir. We're from the gas company. Got to do some safety tests. The law says you have to let us in. You know the standard fine? Let us in or I'm afraid we'll have to cut the gas off. You wouldn't want that, would you?'

Mr Hansen was just about flipping his lid. 'Okay, okay, I'm an architect myself, you don't have to tell me about it. Come in and get on with it. You can start upstairs in the bathroom!'

'Thanks – that saves us a lot of trouble.'

Here we go, thought Greg, without even an internal grin. Pa blustering away, doesn't have a clue how little he knows about human nature. I knew *their* game at once – though it's only since I changed shape I've been able to sense these things so clearly.

Just a few minutes later, he turned out to be perfectly right. Mr Hansen did his best to lure Greg into the dining-room, where there were no gas fittings at all, with the freshest of lettuces and many soothing words, but the men in grey overalls knew their job: check the bathroom, take a look in the kitchen, swift tour of the basement, and as soon as Mr Hansen was busy on his mobile phone again they seized their chance – open the door of the spare bedroom, the living-room, the lavatory, and last of all the dining-room . . .

Click, click, click . . . click, click, click. Toolboxes can easily hold cameras too.

Before anyone but Greg realised exactly what sort of people had wormed their way into the house, the vital photos of the evidence had been taken.

'Come on, let's get moving!'

'Here, let's see your proof of identity?'

'What are you shouting like that for, Thomas?'

'You think my son-in-law needs any help, Helen?'

'Like me to follow them, Pa?'

The house was in chaos. Greg thought it would be rather a good idea to take refuge in his own room.

Next day, Ben came home from school at lunch-time brandishing a newspaper.

'Hey, get a load of this! Want to see some photos of our house? They're dead good.'

The next shock-horror announcement wasn't long in coming either.

'Switch the box on! They're showing this house on the news. They've got pictures of the chase too . . .'

'This can't go on!' said Mr Hansen, watching the news bulletin. 'I'll have to do something about it!'

The next few days were not comfortable for Greg. He was beginning to feel as if his skin was too tight again. His appetite gradually died down. His whole body ached. And a sense of indifference spread through his mind too, like a fog, blurring all his perceptions and his ability to think for himself. He registered the frantic atmosphere both inside and around the house, and certain impressions drifted into his room like wisps of mist – but then they dissolved and drifted away again; there was nothing he could really get hold of.

Perhaps I'm turning non-human entirely, and when I'm all animal maybe life will look different, dreamed the caterpillar.

Sure enough, his keen hearing was still reacting best – to the blackbirds singing at daybreak, to all the birds twittering in the early evening. But the barking that he heard from time to time, always from the same direction, made the caterpillar very, very uneasy, although he didn't want to stop and think about that too much right now.

Now and then Ben cleaned up after him as necessary, clearing away the large, gleaming black balls of dung almost without protest – in fact, there weren't so many of them now – and telling Greg a whole load of weird stuff he'd picked up off the Internet.

'Listen, you're obviously the only one of your kind anywhere in the world . . . But there's any number of other exotic creatures about – with two feet, with eight feet, fifteen feet, one wing, two wings, three wings. With hermaphrodite genitals, meaning half and half, and bisexual, and asexual. With no voices but good hearing. With voices and hearing. With hearing and no intelligence. With intelligence and no penis . . . You know something? The world's full of absolutely crazy creatures, you take my word for it, and dear little mutated brotherkins is right in there with the rest of them. Want to bet you're going to be world famous?'

Greg found monologues like this quite entertaining. His parents came in now and then as well. Mrs Hansen had gone back to trying out Bach flower remedies – also a lot of well-meant remarks.

'I'm to give you special love from Grandfather. He's feeling very weak and has to stay in bed. I'm really worried about him, though he seems perfectly calm himself. He takes this – this change in your shape as if it was perfectly natural, something like flu. Can you hear what I'm telling you?'

Greg's reaction was neither positive nor negative. It was nice to hear Ma's voice. That would do for now.

'Oh, I do hope he's going to be all right. And you too. Maybe it isn't mere chance you're both in this state just now – there always was a special bond between you. I know you men don't hold with that sort of thing, or very few of you anyway, but I'm trying to see all this as the workings of Providence. I've been reading a lot about metamorphosis and reincarnation and similar phenomena. I really believe in them, and I keep trying to tune in to you as hard as I can to pick up your vibes. I'm transmitting positive energies to you day and night, and I'm absolutely sure it will all end well!'

It's a mercy Pa can't hear any of that, thought Greg in his foggy cocoon. He felt an urgent need to be alone again.

Mr Hansen came visiting too, but he kept a safe distance between himself and the caterpillar.

'I'm to give you Sara Auster's best wishes. She says to get well soon!'

Greg lay under his desk with his head drawn in. Sara! He absorbed every word, and immediately the churned-up feelings he'd had before came over him again.

'She said she used to meet you at the school bus stop, and she'd like to come and visit the invalid, but of course I said no, for obvious reasons. Oh, why am I going on like this? As if you . . .'

Mr Hansen broke off in mid-sentence, looked at the caterpillar and shook his head.

'No. No, this is useless.'

Half an hour later Mr Hansen turned up again – and this time he had someone else with him.

'There it is!' Mr Hansen pointed at Greg.

'Very striking. Not unattractive.'

'It usually eats all day – and it eats most at night.'

'We can make something of that. That doesn't come over in the photographs.'

'At the moment it's in one of its introverted phases. Could be a reaction to all the recent turmoil.'

'Reactions resembling human emotions always arouse sympathy. Subconsciously, people like to recognise themselves in other animals.'

'It seems to me you and your people would deal with it well.'

What on earth, wondered Greg in some confusion, what on earth is going on here? His consciousness was clouded, but he recognised his father's voice. Who did the other voice belong to, though? It sounded very strange, and he didn't like it. In fact, it turned him right over.

'Could you just stimulate it a bit, Mr Hansen? Get it to make a few movements? The livelier and more amusing they are, the wider the range of marketing opportunities open to us. Now, if we could appeal to children and young people alike, and extend it to adults too – that would be ideal. That would have the clients just about eating out of our hands, yours and ours – ha, ha, ha!'

Mr Hansen cautiously approached the desk. He seemed to sense that Greg was not enjoying this scene.

'Like something to eat, Gregor?'

You're not here, I'm not here, that other man certainly isn't here! Such were the thoughts that went through Greg's mind. He decided to play dead. A dead caterpillar. But the protective hairs along his sides, and the little red cornicle at his far end, seemed to have a life of their own. His father jumped back.

'Sorry, Mr van Kock,' said Mr Hansen, in some embarrassment. 'It . . . er . . . it seems he doesn't want to play just now. That unpleasant smell is one way of saying so. Like . . . er . . . certain other of his anal and oral peculiarities.'

'Well, we can use all that. Clients like something a

bit naughty these days. There are hardly any taboos now, and we have to use that attitude – we can't ignore it, know what I mean?'

'But no force, mind! And all entirely within the law. I don't want any trouble with the Society for the Protection of Animals, and so forth. And to tell you the truth, Mr van Kock, in spite of all the stress and trouble it's given us, I'm rather fond of the creature. So is my wife.'

'Mr Hansen, you're dealing with a professional who is also a tender-hearted human being. If we do business, you will find you're in the best of hands with us. Of course we'll provide psychological veterinary care. We also regularly observe all the conventions and practices usual in this area of marketing. Your caterpillar will be very well off, and so, of course, will you and I. We'll continue this discussion later at my agency, right, Mr Hansen?'

'Okay.'

'I'll very soon have a complete marketing concept outlined, and then I'll put it to you. It will include a special plan of strategy for dealing with the media. And of course it will include our contract, with all the financial clauses. I think we're all going to get along very well together, my dear Mr Hansen. Opportunities like this don't usually come more than once in a lifetime!'

'One last question, Mr van Kock: do you know a certain Dr Markstein? Director of the Institute of Genetics? He's said to be an eminent authority in his field.'

'I know him by name, yes. He has an international reputation. But I'd leave him out of this if I were you. He'd only put a spanner in the works – he could poach on our preserves. No, an exclusive contract or no contract at all, that's how I see it.'

'I entirely understand. I'm acquainted with the same kind of thing in my own line of business.'

The two voices died away somewhere, just as Greg lost control over himself. His skin was stretched taut to bursting point. His body began to twitch from front to back, first slowly, then more and more violently. A pang, a liberating pang, ran over his outer skin. Then the skin split, and Greg finally fell into the deep sleep of exhaustion.

When he woke from the depths of that sleep, Greg felt reborn. He stretched out to his full length. He wanted to do something. He felt big and strong and, of course, he was ravenously hungry yet again.

'Ma, Pa, come up here, quick! Come and look at this! Hey, talk about an amazing, way-out biological phenomenon!'

Ben was there first, admiring the new Greg.

'Wow, just look at you! You're getting sexier all the time.'

Greg heard his parents come into the room.

'See that, green and yellow!' said Ben. 'He ought to be on telly. Mimicry, that's what they call it. He could play for Brazil in the World Cup!'

By now Greg was in the middle of another vegetarian meal. As he munched and chewed, he enjoyed Ben's remarks – such fraternal praise did him good.

But his parents' grim silence didn't. It bothered Greg. What were they planning? He knew this kind of atmosphere from the old days. It was always a sure sign that something was about to change, surprisingly and usually dramatically.

'Can I have his old skin? I'd like to hang it up in my room as a souvenir, okay?'

No reaction. Just silence.

A *souvenir*?

Greg interrupted his meal. He felt an urge to rear up on end and look in the direction of the place where he could see the dark outlines of his parents standing.

'Oh, do stop crying, Helen!'

No sooner had Pa said her name than Ma sobbed out loud.

'Oh, Ma . . .' Even Ben felt he had to comfort her.

'It's for his own good. You can visit him any time. They'll look after him very well indeed, and I bet he'll enjoy it. I mean, you know what his sort are like. Small and shy on the outside, but they enjoy life in their own quiet way.'

'We can't be responsible for this. Perhaps he needs his home. Nobody can see into his mind.'

'He can come back here any time,' Ben added.

'What, and put us through all this stress again? Tons of salad vegetables. Kilos of caterpillar dung. And these fits of his from time to time. With Paul so ill. Sensation-seeking reporters prowling around the house day and night, robbing us of any private life. Fifty phone calls today alone! Not to mention the faxes, the e-mails, and the stuff that comes by ordinary snail-mail.'

'Stop it, oh, do stop it!' sobbed Mrs Hansen.

'Think of the rest of us, will you? Ben's supposed to take his GCSEs this year. You wanted to start out in your new career. And if I remember correctly I once had a job myself – a job that's supposed to earn us some money, right?'

'Please, Thomas, it's not that . . .'

'Tell us what it is, then, Ma. Spit it out!' said Ben, joining in again.

'I don't want us to do anything wrong. I mean, he's still my child. Or that's how I feel about him, anyway.'

'Look, Ma, parents can't ever be right. Just leave him alone and let him eat in peace – he needs to stoke up for his big show.'

Big show?

This was all too much for Greg, and he was glad to be left in peace. He'd never found it easy to come to terms with his mother's tears, and there was absolutely nothing you could do about Pa when he was all stressed out like this.

Five

It happened next morning. No need for anyone to say anything, to try explaining – Greg knew he'd have to leave home.

That night, when everyone else was asleep – or pretending to be asleep, anyway – he had crawled up and downstairs again: it was boring, and he felt shut in. Since the last time he shed his skin in particular, he felt he was itching to learn something entirely new.

The main thing was to get out of this boring house! Smell different smells, hear different voices, think other . . . well, anyway, get away from the constant complaints about stress and strain. And away from Grandfather Paul.

Why, Greg wondered, did he want to get away from him? But he already knew the answer: I don't want to see him so ill. I want to remember him when he was still fit and well.

Saying goodbye to Sara was different. Greg would have liked to make another excursion to the Austers' house. He had already thought up various ways of dealing with that yapping little Dogmatix. But a gloomy sort of feeling told him he might as well forget any such plan. Things never turn out the way you expect. Who said that? Never mind – the saying promptly proved true when it came to saying goodbye to Ben.

'Here, come into my room! I've got something for you,' said his brother. He was never usually allowed into that room! Ben offered him an open bag of extra-large jelly babies.

'But no messes in here, okay? Here, you have these, and don't think too badly of me, right? I'll look after Sara, try cheering her up a bit.'

Plop! Oh – !

Greg really hadn't meant to, but that last remark brought it all up again: the cassette, his jealousy, his guilty conscience, throwing up the broken bits . . .

'Oh no, what did I tell you?' Only now did Ben spot Greg's black offering. 'It's about time someone house-trained you. Go on, get out of here, before I get scabies or something!'

Greg was glad to comply.

You just wait, he thought, you'll get the surprise of

your lives! And he realised he was suffering from something like stage-fright.

This presentiment soon turned out to be accurate. Greg had crawled down to the front door of his own accord, unasked. By now the racket down there and the confused voices shouting outside the house were nothing new. But the bright light shining through the glass did confuse the caterpillar.

He heard his mother's strained voice. 'Do we have to have all this fuss?'

'This is the age of the media, Helen. The press and TV people aren't going to walk away from a story like this. It'll soon be over.'

Mr Hansen's mobile phone rang. An attractive female voice spoke. 'We're ready now. You think our star will go along with the performance?'

'Just a moment!' Mr Hansen leaned down to Greg. 'You'd like to go for an outing with us, right? Don't be afraid of all those people out there. It's only natural for them to want to see something amazing like you. Can you understand what I'm saying?'

What utter twaddle!

'Oh, let him out!' said Ben. 'If you ask me, he's going to enjoy it.'

The front door opened. Greg was dazzled. There was

a lot of clicking, and a few people applauded.

The friendly voice Greg had heard on the mobile phone was quite close to him now. 'Come along, beautiful! We have a nice surprise for you.'

Interestingly, it wasn't the crisp, fresh lettuce that tempted Greg to follow, but the scent of the young woman who had spoken to him. Something about her reminded him of Sara. Something or other was luring him into an adventure that he still couldn't envisage properly.

'Careful – up the ramp here and on to the loading platform,' the voice told him.

Another voice spoke up, also female but nothing like as pleasant. It was carrying on in a way he found very confusing.

'Well, viewers, here we are at last! Exclusive – live – for the first time ever, in all its glory, and tame and docile too: the amazing giant caterpillar! We've been holding our breath for days, waiting to see it ... the first of its species ever known anywhere in the world ... not cloned, not any kind of double ... and right now it's on its way to the studio ... we'll keep the outside cameras on it, it won't be out of your sight for a second ... you can watch every stage in its journey from the comfort of your own home ... so don't switch off, because we'll be back with you live after the break!'

What's going on? Where am I?

Greg was agitated. Greg was confused. But he was also just a little proud to be the centre of so much sudden attention. He took every step very deliberately, thinking about it for the first time in quite a while: last pair of legs, next pair of legs, next pair of legs, then everything forward! Bend and stretch, bend and . . .

'That's great, Greggy. Now, we're going for a little drive in this van, and there's a real caterpillar paradise waiting for you at the end of the journey.'

More applause. A door was closed. The engine started . . .

'Stop! Turn that engine off. Open up this van! We are confiscating that caterpillar. We have official authorisation to take it away for special investigation.'

Sounds like something out of a crime story, thought Greg. He didn't want part of any of this; his appetite had suddenly revived, and he had to obey it. The female person beside him seemed to understand all about that; she was holding lettuce leaves right in front of his quietly scrunching jaws.

There were now violent arguments going on outside the van. The TV reporter woman was transmitting live again. Pa had come out of the house. Two men in civilian clothes were waving a piece of paper in front of his nose.

'We have to take this animal away. It's a danger to public safety. It must be kept at the Institute of Genetics under official supervision and control until we have an expert opinion on it.'

'Gentlemen, you've made a mistake. I must ask you to leave at once! This is my private house, and the creature in that van is my private property.'

Private property?

'My baby, so to speak. Call it anything you like – but keep your hands off it!'

'We're speaking to Mr Thomas Hansen, is that right?'

'Yes, it is, and any further communication will be through my solicitor. He lives just over there, the other side of this field, and I'll be happy to give you the address and phone number of his office.'

'So here we go, viewers – a live TV sensation. A real-life, totally unscripted event! Let us assure you that Greggy is doing just fine in that van. Our qualified veterinarian psychologist Lizzie will be looking after the wonderful giant caterpillar, and I'm sure he'll be really enjoying all the excitement. Now, I guess you're as curious as I am to see what's going on back at the studio right now – have they finished preparations for our special Greggy Park yet? Let's go over to the Greggy studio!'

Am I dreaming or is this real?

Right now, Greg felt as if his chief responsibility was to his enormous stomach, but he couldn't entirely blank out the media circus going on around him.

'Relax – we'll be off in a moment,' said Lizzie's soothing voice.

Sure enough, after some to-ing and fro-ing and a couple of extremely audible remarks from Mr Hansen, the van began to move.

Greg's sense of time wasn't functioning, and he didn't really mind, but at some point the van stopped, although the show went on:

'Well, you kids out there – all you viewers young and old! We know you've been eagerly waiting for this moment for days, and here we are at last: Greggy's right here with us now! After long and complex negotiations, we're able to present you with this sensation live, exclusive – right here and now, wow, what a thrill! Here comes the amazing caterpillar, making straight for our special Greggy studio! You'll never believe what you're about to see – and if there's anyone out there wants to enrich their lives with a brand-new experience, we'll be back on the air right after the break!'

Enrich their lives with what brand-new experience?

'Come on, dear, don't let all this noise bother you.

There honestly is quite a surprise waiting for you in there – they've made it very comfortable for you. I've checked everything out, and it really is caterpillar heaven!'

Greg listened to the nice voice and drank in Lizzie's fragrance. Nothing and no one else, apart from Sara, had ever seemed so captivating. How old would she be? Twenty, twenty-five? Maybe even as old as thirty?

How come he felt so good with her, so safe? As he crawled down the ramp, Greg felt really sorry, for the first time in ages, that he didn't have a clear view of the person he was following.

'Hi there, viewers, here we come! Greggy is on his way. He'll be in the studio any moment now. Everything's ready for him there – he'll want for nothing. As you can see – plenty of room for exercise, more than he'd get in any zoo. Bright, attractive toys specially chosen for every mood a caterpillar might feel. And, of course, the very best of fresh food, and always on hand to look after him there's our specialist in animal behaviour and animal psychology, Lizzie here! Welcome – welcome to the Greggy Park!'

The place was bright with floodlights. It was pleasantly warm, although there was a peculiar smell. Greggy went the way they wanted him to go, and found himself entering a truly huge room, fitted out with some genuine bushes and trees and with papier-mâché hills, rocks and stones, and all kinds of other stuff. Greg could just make out some of the shapes with his wide-angled eyes. Some of it had a nice smell, a smell he already knew, some of it smelled very artificial or as if it had only just been painted.

'So welcome to our live show, Greggy! Welcome to your caterpillar paradise! My name's Gina, and now I'll hand you over to Lizzie, our special animal behaviourist, who will be personally caring for Greggy.'

'Well ... hello, everyone here in the studio and everyone watching from home. First I'd like to say I'm really excited, and I'm sure Greggy feels the same. This is the first time either of us has faced all these cameras and microphones. Maybe everyone wants to be on TV at some point in their lives, and I can assure you that Greggy is enjoying the wonderful reception you're giving him.'

Plop!

Greg had no idea where he had just relieved himself. All these sense impressions at once made him almost giddy. Also, being called Greggy all the time was getting him down.

'As you can see, our attractive friend with all those pairs of legs has already marked his territory. He seems to feel happy here – isn't that right, Greggy?'

Greg realised he was being addressed, and he became aware of the small, round thing being held in front of him. He wondered briefly whether a belch might be the right response, but decided to save it for later. He was hungry, and he wanted to get out of this glaring light.

'Interviewing isn't always easy! Greggy knows what he wants – he has a will of his own, and we must respect it. He needs time to settle into his new home and learn his way around.'

New home?

What were they going on about? How on earth do *they* think they know what I want?

Before Greg could find the answer to any of that, he discovered something else: lovely crisp, fresh lettuce in a shady place . . .

'Hi, friends, hi there, fans!' The overexcited presenter Gina again. 'Well, now, I guess we ought to let Greggy have a little peace and quiet. But our cameras will be here the whole time, so you won't miss a thing. Meanwhile, this is your chance to ask questions, tell us your own opinions, say what you'd like to see on the programme. You can reach us by phone, fax or e-mail, and of course there's our Internet home page where you'll find the very latest about Greggy, all the most important facts. We'll be adding news flashes the moment they come in. Well, we'll be back on the air

directly after the break with the super-Greggy game –
amazing prizes, and of course a chance to visit the
studio yourself! So take care, bye now, see you in a
minute.'

Greg had eaten his fill, and he felt exhausted. He
urgently needed a little nap. A nap up on one of the
studio trees, where no one could disturb him. With his
head drawn in to protect him from the floodlights. And
coiled up, because sleeping coiled up made a caterpillar
feel good.

Six

When Greg woke up again it was night. All was quiet in the big studio. Some of the floodlights had been switched off, and there was no sign of the overexcited presenter, or Lizzie either. However, Greg felt he was under observation. Whether he was doing a few gymnastic exercises and a little climbing on the tree where he'd had his nap, just to limber up again, or whether he was looking for something to eat among the bushes, there always seemed to be an eye of some kind following him around.

Greg's brain suddenly clicked into gear. Automatic cameras, it said.

How did you deal with those?

Just ignore them, Greg decided. The main thing is I can move about freely. And that was fun, especially his expeditions up the tall studio walls and in between the struts on which the floodlights were mounted. The large balls of dung that Greg dropped to the floor from time to time made a wonderful sploshing, plopping noise – this is the life, thought Greg. This is the life for a caterpillar! He was feeling good.

It was some hours before the studio came to life again. The first to reappear was Lizzie. Greg knew her first from the way she walked, and then from her fragrance. She stayed waiting to one side, and Greg felt her eyes watching him.

He felt embarrassment ... How come I feel embarrassed?

Memories surfaced, but Greg wanted no more to do with feelings of that kind. I'll just say hi, he decided, crawling her way.

'Hello, my friend the TV star! How do you like your paradise? Any complaints? Ready for your next appearance?'

Greg liked the friendly way she talked to him, and he felt sorry he couldn't say anything back. Then Lizzie did something else. It took Greg by surprise at first, but then it made him feel really good: she stroked his head, very gently, very tenderly, very lovingly...

Don't stop, he tried signalling, don't stop! But people were now crowding busily into the studio.

'Hey, so this is our monster!'

'Very tame, our shooting star.'

'Ooh, isn't it just sweet!'

Greg noticed Lizzie making signs to the film crew to keep quiet.

Floodlights came on. Requests to check microphones and cameras came over the loudspeakers. A director issued instructions from somewhere overhead. The studio set was adjusted, and before long Gina took over again in her bright, youthful, excitable voice.

'Hi, darlings, everyone okay? How's our amazing caterpillar doing? I can see he's in good hands, so let's begin.'

'Ready to go on air!' The loud command echoed through the studio. Suddenly Greg had stage-fright again. He was about to draw his head in when Lizzie whispered, 'Don't worry, they only want to know you're all right. Look, I guess it would be a good idea for you to start feeding if they can find you something.'

He was certainly hungry. Tremendously hungry. Ravenously hungry.

Greg now remembered that at some point in the night he'd gone looking for something fresh to eat, in vain, and then he'd fallen asleep exhausted.

'Camera!'

'Hi, kids – and I wouldn't be surprised if you were bunking off school on purpose to see our show! Hi there, everyone, large and small! Welcome to our Greggy Park, live and exclusive, on this channel only! Greggy says hi too! Greggy says good morning! Lizzie has been looking after him very well. Greg feels bright as a button, he's on fine form, and now of course he's ready for his breakfast – you can watch him eat it live!'

A man with a salesman's smile, a basket of vegetables, and two brightly coloured packets of something in his hand entered the studio, walking jauntily and making straight for Greg.

'Now, quite a number of you have already called or faxed, you've sent good wishes, you've asked questions and said you'd like to visit the studios here. So right after Greggy's breakfast we'll move over to the audience studio and switch you through live. It's all live here, no recordings, no cuts – you're right here with us and Greggy, our own unique, sensational caterpillar! So enjoy your breakfast.'

'And let's hope our studio guest enjoys his,' said the smiling man. 'The very best fresh lettuce – but first, here's something that does our treasured pets at home so much good! It should always be a part of their breakfast. Here we are: Medi-Vital! And to make sure your pets have no problems, give them a Mega-Vital after every meal – all made from guaranteed plant substances, laboratory tested, internationally approved!'

Belch!

The smiling salesman character flinched, and Lizzie couldn't help grinning.

'Well, as you all know, pets are inclined to behave unpredictably! They do their own thing. Maybe we'd better start with the lettuce, and then – '

Gina the presenter intervened: 'And then we'll go straight over to the studio audience. But first, a few important tips for the day. Don't miss anything, don't switch off, because everything on this channel will be presented by the nation's darling – Greggy, the giant caterpillar!'

'Wait! Stop! This won't do! This is just so amateurish! You're not promoting sales, you're preventing them!'

That voice! Yes, it *was* Mr van Kock – no doubt about it, here comes Mr van Kock again!

Greg had already found that the preceding conversation got on his nerves or, anyway, on his little red cornicle. He couldn't help it: that small red excrescence had just given off some of its own unmistakable poisonous smell.

'Come with me, dear. I think all this is rather stressful for you. Look, there's a quiet place where you could feed at the back here. Have some nice lettuce.'

Greg did as Lizzie said. He felt hot and dizzy, and

most of all he felt very, very hungry.

'I really do think we ought to take it easy with him. He has to get used to his new home first.'

These words from Lizzie were all that Greg felt inclined to register: he was deaf to everything else said by anyone at all over the next few hours.

He ate and he ate and he defecated.

He made his way through the greenery of the studio set, some of which, unfortunately, turned out to be fake. Finally, he drew his head in and was nothing but a body. Without thought, without a past, without a future.

'Ooh, look, isn't it sweet!'

'Look at them lovely colours!'

'Can we touch it?'

Greg was brought back to the present by the carryings-on in the studio. It was like being at the zoo or the circus. There were dozens of children milling around not far from him, marvelling at the sight.

'Not too close, please, children. And not so loud! Greggy may be a vegetarian, I mean a tame caterpillar who eats only plants, but you never know . . .'

Too right, thought Greg, putting out his head. He uncoiled and stretched.

There was much screeching and running about.

'Well, hi there, all you Greggy fans here in the studio and watching at home! This is what we've been waiting for, this is what we've been really looking forward to! Our amazing caterpillar is waking up. I wonder what he feels like doing after that lovely long sleep? Whatever it is, we'll show it to you live, exclusive. So don't switch off! After some important information on our competition game and the very latest Greggy products, we'll be back here in the Greggy Park ... with lots of studio guests, and plenty of surprises!'

She can keep her surprises! thought Greg, setting off in the direction of the presenter. Her voice is so shrill, and she talks such nonsense. I really have to make that clear to her!

To the delight of the children, he crawled straight towards Gina's perfume, unerringly and with remarkable speed.

'There, kiddiwinks, see that? Our Greggy's feeling just fine. He has everything he could wish for in his paradise. Everybody loves him. Everybody's spoiling him rotten. And everybody just loves his clever ideas.'

More shouting and running about. There was something Greg wanted to find out for sure. Although he could sense that the presenter was no longer feeling very happy herself, he moved very close to her.

'Ooh ... I wonder what Greggy wants now? He's never tried to get so close to anyone before. Help! What's the idea, caterpillar?'

I want to eat you, Greg would have liked to announce through the nearest microphone, I want to eat you! As the studio guests squealed, he reared his front segments up, somehow or other got a grip on the brightly coloured bits of plastic that were Gina's skirt, and tried to climb up on her lap.

'Help, Lizzie! This is going too far! I'm scared!'

'Greggy, come on, please. Don't flirt with our nice presenter, she's already engaged to someone else. Look, here's something nice for you to eat ...'

Plop!

Greg dropped a large, black, gleaming ball of dung right in front of Gina's feet as a goodbye present.

'Yeeeuuk!'

'Watch his face!'

Greg was pleased: if he was destined to be a TV star then he might as well go the whole way! He ate some of the fresh lettuce with relish, turned away from the nervous Gina, and climbed a tree.

'Yes, this is live TV, the real thing!' said the presenter, audibly subdued. 'Well, enjoy the other tricks Greggy has to show you. There are five cameras recording everything he does. And I'm announcing a

Greggy Special this evening. On our great Saturday night show – plenty of music, plenty of games, plenty of studio guests. So stay with us, don't switch off, and you won't regret it.'

Greg was glad when the studio was finally quiet again. The children had been sent home with a Greggy Special goody-bag apiece, and the presenter had been whispering agitatedly to Lizzie in a corner. Greg had picked up every word.

'I don't trust that creature. I think he's got it in for me.'

'Honestly, I think he's harmless,' said Lizzie. 'But what I say doesn't go for much. Less stress would be better for him. He's a nocturnal creature, and being exposed to cameras all day long – well, we'd none of us like that, would we?'

'Tell that to the director and the management team. They've thought it all through logically. They'll never have another chance like this to get the station out of the red!'

'I'm starting to feel sorry for him. He's more sensitive than any of us thought. There's sometimes a feeling around him that unsettles me. It's not like with any normal animal. Do you know what I mean?'

'No,' said the presenter. 'I don't. And what I need

right now is something for my poor nerves.'

Same here, thought Greg, tucking into the salads. He had this empty feeling inside him almost all the time, and another feeling too: a sense that something very unusual was about to happen. He had to eat and eat to be able to deal with it. Life was getting more and more exciting – well, he had no objection to that.

Greg's premonitions soon proved to be well founded. Early that evening, stage-hands began converting the studio. They brought in chairs and sofas. They put up a platform for musicians. They also erected stands with outsize caterpillar photographs. They distributed lavish flower arrangements all over the place, not forgetting ads for any number of Greggy products, all available on the market in the very near future.

Greg himself wanted nothing to do with all this fuss. He enjoyed his constitutional up the studio walls and over the studio sets. As he crawled around, he noticed that most of the studio staff had taken to keeping a good distance away from him. Obviously his attentions to the nervous Gina had earned him their respect.

And then something happened. Lizzie came in search of Greg. She sat down in front of him and did something no one but his mother had ever done before. Lizzie looked at him long and hard. She concentrated, and in that silence she made contact with him. Greg couldn't pull himself away. Then, at last, she started talking to him gently.

'Listen, dear. I know you really like people – you do like human company, don't you?'

Depends whose it is, Greg wanted to say.

He lay at his carer's feet, absorbing her pleasant, appealing fragrance, even feeling the warmth of her body.

'Now, some people you know are coming here this evening. Of course the TV people hope you'll play along with them a bit. All I really want to say is that there's nothing for you to worry about. I'll stay close to you all the time, keeping an eye on you. And remember, everyone here likes you, even if they do sometimes talk rubbish.'

Rubbish it is, too. This comment was on the tip of Greg's jaws, but it couldn't get out. Instead, rather to his surprise, he succeeded in producing a perfectly timed belch.

'Okay, I get the idea!' said Lizzie promptly, and she left Greg alone.

Seven

Evening came, and Greg felt nervous. All the fuss and kerfuffle had numbed his senses, and he couldn't think clearly. He felt like hiding behind part of the studio set to watch his own show. On the other hand, suddenly finding yourself a big TV star did have its advantages.

'Okay, everyone in position! Camera ready? Sound ready? Lizzie, try to get our beloved pet there over to the guest sofa, would you?'

And then the show was on air. A group opened the transmission with a real scorcher of a song. The cone of a spotlight followed Greg as he crawled over to the sofa. The presenter, Gina, was standing in another spot. She announced, in tones of hectic cheerfulness, 'Hi, friends! Hi, all you fans out there! Welcome to the Greggy Park on prime-time TV! Only on this channel – live, in person – this amazing biological sensation, a source of fascination to all scientists and experts, visible proof that we're entering a new age, a new millennium – Greggy the gigantic giant caterpillar!'

I don't feel all that gigantic, thought Greg, making his way over to the guests' podium beside Lizzie. Still, let's see what kind of a show they're putting on today.

'And what interests us all most? Who would we really like to see here, live, in the studio? Well, obviously our star's parents, or whatever you like to call them. And Greggy's brother too, of course. And they're right here now – not caterpillars, not butterflies, as you may be thinking, no, perfectly ordinary, normal people on two legs! Mr and Mrs Hansen and Greggy's brother, Ben!'

Greg froze. He had dimly guessed what was coming, but he still felt upset. This was distressing, and he wondered whether he should run for it, or rather crawl for it – get out of this spotlight as fast as possible.

'Oh – I see my announcement wasn't quite correct. There's one person missing, but all the same, I'm delighted we can have this chat with Mr and Mrs Hansen. It's a shame Greggy can't take any active part, but here he is, in all his attractive, unique colours!'

'Come on, dear, here's some fresh food!' Lizzie was enticing the now anxious Greg over to the couch. 'Eat up – I'll stay here with you.'

That smell . . . that voice!

At the same time, and a little way off, Greg saw the shadowy forms of the two people who were so familiar to him, and yet now seemed so strange and far away.

'You know, viewers, I'm really moved by this first reunion! It's just so touching! I suggest we leave the family alone for a few minutes. I have some important information, very useful for your next shopping trip, and of course there's the Greggy competition with terrific opportunities and attractive prizes. Don't miss it, don't switch off – we'll be back in the studio after the break!'

Greg was getting sick and tired of her shrill, penetrating voice. But when his mother came up to him, that was really exciting.

'Greggy! Oh, Greggy, how are you?'

'Hi, Gregor. You're looking well,' said his father.

That seemed to be it. Greg could sense how shy and awkward his mother was feeling, and his father's voice sounded as if he were talking to some business acquaintance with whom he wasn't entirely at ease.

I can't seem to get the hang of this, said Greg to himself, and he decided to have something to eat instead.

'Hi there, friends! Hi there, Greggy fans! Here we are back again, and now I'd like to ask my guests a few

128

questions. But first – oh, I really can't wait, I just have to know – what happened to Greggy's brother? Where's Ben?'

'I'm afraid he's not well,' said Mr Hansen. 'He had to stay in bed.'

'Dear me – I expect his little brother's rise to fame was too much for his digestion! Well, Ben, if you're watching, get well soon! And now we come to the main subject – Mrs Hansen, or may I call you Helen? Helen, how does it feel when your son suddenly disappears overnight, and you find a handsome caterpillar there instead?'

Mrs Hansen looked at Greg. She seemed upset.

'To tell you the truth I still haven't really taken it in. I can't sleep at night. It's like a dream, a nightmare, and then I see him like this and ... well, it may sound funny, but he's still my child.'

'And how about you, Thomas? How do you feel about this strange situation?'

'I'm a rationalist. In my profession I'm used to tackling and solving concrete, practical problems. So here I am, facing this thing that's happened. I really feel rather the same way as my wife: I'm waiting for the moment when the dream's over. I just can't believe it.'

'And Thomas, Helen – what did it? What caused this metamorphosis? That's what all the viewers calling us and faxing us want to know: how can a thing like this happen?'

'We've no more idea than anyone else,' said Mrs Hansen. 'We've talked to medical and zoological experts, and they're all baffled. I . . . I'm just desp – '

Here Mrs Hansen began sobbing, and Greg had to stop eating. Mr Hansen spoke up again.

'Right now we have to follow up any theory – nothing can be ruled out entirely. Some of the experts put it down to genetically modified food. Others suggest a mutation as a result of some previously unknown virus that attacks young people at puberty. Others again say it could be some unusual kind of reincarnation, but as a rational, logically-minded engineer I rule that one out!'

'Here – hic! Can I – hic! Let me have a – hic!'

Greg took notice. Even the presenter seemed genuinely surprised for once.

'Viewers, you'll just have to believe me – this new guest has arrived entirely unexpectedly, and first may I know who – '

'My name's Ben. Hic! Hansen. Hic! And this weird little creepy-crawly – hic! Mind, it's not a bad little creepy-crawly – that's my little brother. And I'm – hic! – I'm my little brother's weird little *big* brother – hic!'

'Ben!' whispered Mrs Hansen, astonished, and Ben's

father began shaking his head and couldn't stop.

'Well now, Greggy fans, isn't this amazing – live TV, unscripted, uncut, uncensored! If I'm not much mistaken, Ben Hansen has got out of bed, even though he didn't feel too well, and made his way here to the studio. Am I right?'

'Yup – hic! And I think – hic! – I think I'd better lie down.'

'Ben!' Mrs Hansen tried to stand up, but her husband pushed her back down on the sofa.

'Well, viewers, shall we ask Ben, in spite of his fragile condition, how *he* accounts for his brother's sudden change of shape? Ben, can you tell us anything?'

'Hic.'

Ben had gone over to Greg – or, rather, staggered over to him. He stopped in front of the caterpillar, tried to stand without swaying too much, and looked down at him with a grin.

'Well, little brother, still farting around? I kind of miss you, little one – hic! – yup, I really miss you!'

The presenter had been following Ben with the microphone. Now she tapped him on the shoulder. 'May I repeat my question, Ben? Do *you* have any explanation for this amazing transformation?'

Ben looked at Gina, started swaying again, and then began sniffing and couldn't stop.

'Sorry, lady – it's your perfume, hic! – kind of really strong – hic! But yes, 's an important question, hic! I'd say this is kind of the end of play. We're into extra time – into the third half, if you can have a third half – hic! And him there, he's showing us what the future will be like – hic! He always was a bit crazy, and mad about animals – so now he's showing everyone what he can do – hic! A real monster, hic! I think it's great! Got us all gawping at him, right?'

'Well . . . well, now, viewers, hi there, fans, I guess Ben has given us all something to think about! So now let's give our guests a little rest, shall we? And for them, and all of you, we'll now play our song *Five Greggies* – live, no playback! After that, some hot new consumer info, and then we'll be back on air – with yet another surprise guest! You'll be really amazed, and I'm willing to bet Greggy will too. Bye now, take care, see you soon!'

Plop! But Greg couldn't care less. This sudden encounter with Ben and his parents had him thoroughly confused. He definitely wanted to get out of this.

'Come on, dear, there's more to eat over here,' said Lizzie, soothingly, stroking his long back.

But Greg didn't feel like eating. He had an uneasy feeling in his stomach, one he could hardly bear.

Everything was going round and round in his brain, and his one clear thought was: maybe the alcohol on Ben's breath has got *me* tipsy too!

The break lasted rather longer than planned. The band had to play a couple of extra songs while everyone joined in persuading Ben to leave the studio. He didn't show willing until Mr Hansen whispered something in his ear.

'Okay, boss, I get it! The show must go on without me, hic! But be nice to my little brother, hic! . . . or I plan to turn into a caterpillar too, see?'

Ben was escorted out, and they started preparing for someone else to appear at another door in the studio.

'Hi there again, viewers, hi there, fans! I've just been told that the ratings for this evening's programme have broken all records, and I'm not surprised – everyone wants to see the star of our show. Everyone wants to know more about the background to this amazing phenomenon. And that's why we've invited a very special guest who has something to say that will interest us all. Our very special guest, our special surprise for Greggy himself is – Sara Auster!'

Sara!

Greg thought he must have heard wrong. Sara!

She walked into the studio with a charming smile,

her cheeks pink with excitement. She stopped beside Greg, looked at him intently, and then didn't seem to know where she was supposed to go next.

'Come and sit on the couch with us, would you, Sara dear? Now, for your information, fans and viewers, Sara lives next door to Greg, in a house only a few hundred metres away. Over the last few weeks she's been going to school almost daily in the same school bus as Ben and Greg Hansen – I mean the boy Greg, not Greg the caterpillar. And I know there's something very special Sara is about to tell us! But first, a question for Lizzie, our animal behaviourist. How's Greggy doing? Would it be an idea to give him some Medi-Vital as a tonic? Or what about the tried and trusted Mega-Vital remedy?'

The presenter held both packets up in full view of the camera. Greg was feeling quite faint: he'd expected something might happen – that tingling inside him had never let him down yet – but not this! And Ben was still probably only on the other side of the door. Oh, this was too much!

'Well, Sara, tell us how you got to know the Hansen brothers and, if it's not too intimate a question, what was your relationship with them?'

Sara hesitated, and kept looking at Greg, but he just lay there with his head drawn in – on the outside, he looked as if he were paying no attention to the programme at all, certainly not to this particular interview.

'I don't know if I really ought to tell you . . .'

'Come on, Sara! You can trust us, and maybe you could help to solve this amazing, fascinating Greggy mystery. I mean, what's television for? Where else can we all talk so freely?'

This Gina is a real drag, thought Greg, without moving. If she carries on like that much longer I shall go for her again and make her run away – for good this time!

'I – I noticed Greg from the first day . . . and his brother too,' Sara began. 'I kept waiting for Greg to speak to me.'

'Didn't he take any notice of you, then? Didn't he – well, chat you up, know what I mean?'

'No, Ben chatted me up.'

'So what was your impression of Greg?'

'I thought he was nice. Really nice.'

'Anything in particular about him strike you?'

'Yes, I thought he was special.'

'How do you mean, special? Abnormal, or what?'

'Kind of good looking and nice and very shy.'

'So then?'

'Then we exchanged glances.'

'And?'

'He didn't dare do anything else.'

'So then you turned to Ben?'

Greg suddenly felt hot. He could hardly keep still, but at the same time he had to hear everything – even the worst.

'Well, yes,' said Sara. 'Because I needed him.'

'May we know what for?'

'I wanted to give him a cassette.'

'With music?'

'With music and a guessing game ... and a question.'

'For Ben?'

'No, Greg, of course.'

'I don't quite understand. You'll have to explain to the viewers in more detail.'

Sara said nothing for several moments, looking at Greg, lost in thought.

'You don't need to worry about him. I'm afraid he doesn't understand anything we're saying.'

'All right,' said Sara. 'Okay. I recorded a tape for Greg saying how I felt, and asking him some questions, and then I gave it to his brother Ben to give to him.'

What?

Greg was unable to stay coiled up with his head drawn in any longer.

'So how did Greg react? Did he answer?'

'No . . . it was right after that he . . .' whispered Sara, 'it was right after that it must have happened.'

She began to sob. Mrs Hansen gave her a handkerchief.

Greg heard, and finally he could stand it no longer. He crawled away, fast.

'See how gracefully our Greggy moves, viewers!' said the presenter, turning back to Sara. 'Just one last question, Sara dear: do you really think that – er – that caterpillar's the same Greg you sent the cassette to?'

'Yes. Yes, I do . . .'

Greg had gone to hide in the far corner of the studio, moving as fast as he could. As soon as he got there he regretted it, and thought of crawling back again. In the background he heard Gina's shrill voice carrying on as usual, with new announcements about even more surprises and products and competitions and prizes . . .

By the time Greg finally made up his mind to crawl back, they'd all gone: his mother, his father, Sara and Ben – every last one of them.

Greg spent the next few days in a kind of trance.

Sara. Sara. Sara.

Sara's appearance in the studio kept going round

and round inside Greg's mind, like a video clip playing over and over again.

All those things she'd said! Did she really want to make friends with me from the start? Did she record the cassette for me and not Ben all along?

He'd stored up every word. The sound of Sara's voice, the moment she started crying, everything.

Why didn't I get closer to her? Why did I have to be so stupidly shy?

Greg imagined crazy, hazy, dazy things – not a comic-strip crab and scorpion this time, but two real . . . two real . . . ?

'What's the matter with you, Greggy?' asked Lizzie, not for the first time, disturbing Greg's fantasies.

Since Sara's visit, the caterpillar had avoided her as far as possible. Even the freshest of lettuce and Lizzie's pleasant fragrance couldn't tempt him close, and he shrank from her friendly words and stroking now.

Who knows: perhaps Sara's sitting at home in front of the TV set at this very moment? Perhaps she wants to know how I'm doing here? Maybe she'll come to another show . . . I have to see her again! I do so want to see her again! I'll do everything I can to get her here! Greg determined. But for the time being there were other items on the programme.

'Hi there, kids, hi there, fans, hi, all you friends of

Greggy!' cried the presenter Gina, her voice almost cracking with enthusiasm. 'Today I don't just welcome a teenage audience here to the Greggy Park. I'm also proud to be able to introduce one of our greatest, most famous animal trainers. Here with us now, and soon to be a permanent guest on the show as Greggy's friend – Carino Marino! A big hand for Carino Marino!'

What on earth was going on? What are they planning this time? Greg wondered, climbing high above the studio floor among the struts of the floodlights, much to the enjoyment of the studio guests.

'Hey, look what it's doing up there ... Wow! Terrific! Wicked! Cool!'

'Yes, dear friends and viewers, come and have a good time with us. Our cameras are showing you live, unrecorded, everything our Greggy here gets up to. And now I can announce what we're planning next – we're going to extend the Greggy Paradise and build him an ultra-gigantic Greggy Park. With plenty of room for him to exercise, with lots of attractions – and with other exotic creatures to keep him company! Greggy will feel even better then, and there'll be even more fun for all of you at home! You can find more details on Ceefax and our Web site, and very soon, exclusive to us, in our magazine *Greggy Bravissimo* – every Monday at the newsagents, special price for subscribers. But now, let's move on to the latest consumer info – don't miss it, don't switch off! After the break we'll be right back here in the studio.'

Other exotic creatures? Other? Exotic? Creatures?

Greg didn't like the sound of that. He had no desire at all to be exposed to their entertaining plops and any other home comforts they might offer. He wasn't interested in the Greggy fan club, or the new, ultimate Greggy logo, the Greggy lunch boxes and pencil cases, the towels and pyjamas, the caps and T-shirts and all the rest of it . . . he needed time to think, and he wanted to put as much distance as possible between himself and the excitable Gina.

The next programme transmitted from the studio wasn't calculated to cheer Greg up, either. They'd brought in the guest couch again, and this time they were expecting distinguished visitors.

'Welcome, Greggy fans!' Gina began presenting the show much as usual. 'Today I welcome some illustrious guests, experts in animal conservation, ecologists, churchmen and women, and representatives of the main political parties. And the subject of discussion will be – what else? – our own dear Greggy. We know our caterpillar is happy here! But we also know that some people are concerned about our beloved pet, so of course we're more than willing to give them a hearing. And we're truly, truly sorry that Greggy can't say how he feels about his situation himself. But of course the camera will show how he reacts to our guests during the discussion. So sit back and enjoy this controversial debate! And now I'll hand over to the chairman!'

Anything you say, thought Greg, crawling into the thickest studio bush available. Once there he coiled up, drew his head in, and decided not to listen to another word.

Well, that showed them!

Greg was rather pleased with himself. I'll tackle that silly yackety-yacking woman next, he decided, and the opportunity soon presented itself.

'Hi there, fans, all of you still watching out there! This evening we have something very special for you. You can see one of today's most prominent animal photographers taking pictures of Greggy with his brand new CD camera. And let me tell you what it's in aid of too: very soon now, we'll be issuing the first interactive CD-ROM for our many fans who are computer buffs – with Greggy, about Greggy, even by Greggy! Infotainment, docutainment, edutainment all combined, in compact form on a single CD, exclusive to our channel and presented by your friend Gina here!'

Here there was a plop, followed by a few other noises: Greg had crept up on their friend Gina from behind, successfully taking her by surprise.

'Well, that's live TV for you!' said the presenter, forcing a smile and making off behind the scenes as fast as she could go.

'My nerves won't stand this much longer,' Gina told Lizzie during the next break in transmission. 'See the horrible way that creature's glaring at me?'

For once, Greg stuck around to overhear their conversation.

'That's not his real face – he just uses it for camouflage,' Lizzie explained.

'Well, it scares me all the same,' said the presenter crossly. 'He follows me around in my dreams. Sometimes I think he isn't real at all, sometimes I think those Hansens are pulling a fast one ... I mean, whoever heard of a child changing shape like this! Maybe an extra-terrestrial dropped in on them, and now they're making money out of it.'

Ho, yes, ET, that's me! I have extra-terrestrial urges and all, thought Greg, amused. And he felt the cornicle at his far end beginning to stir of its own accord again.

'I mean, look at that thing there!' cried Gina,

holding her nose. 'Any moment now he'll give off that horrible smell and stink us out.'

Lizzie couldn't suppress a smile. 'It's his cornicle, and perfectly normal,' she explained. 'Don't you think all this may be too much for him?'

'That caterpillar has to be tamed and got under control or I'm handing in my notice!' said Gina, giving herself a little shake. 'How come the top brass here have let that vulture van Kock outmanoeuvre them? Did you hear what they're planning for this brute?'

Brute? Did she really call me that?

Greg lost his temper. He had to defend himself – he'd give this stupid cow a lesson.

'Watch out!' Lizzie warned.

Greg reared up until he was standing on only his eight hind legs, cracked his jaws as loud as he could, and let his bright red cornicle do its stuff.

'Help! Carino Marino, where are you?' cried Gina, staring horrified into the terrifying camouflage face.

'Really, he isn't dangerous – I promise you!' Lizzie tried to soothe her.

But Greg didn't seem to agree. He started moving towards the presenter as fast as his little legs would allow.

'Help! Help!' screeched Gina, without moving from the spot.

Several studio workers came running in, and Lizzie cried, 'Greggy, watch out, we're on air! If Sara sees you like this . . .'

That stopped Greg in his tracks. He couldn't go on with it. All the excitement was suddenly over. He turned away from Gina's overpowering perfume. He just wanted to go away and hide.

'Take it easy – come over here,' said Lizzie soothingly.

But Greg was already on his way to the far corner of the studio. Everyone watched him, transfixed. They suddenly seemed greatly impressed by this extra-ordinary creature who could express his feelings so well without words.

'Things can't go on like this,' said Lizzie, looking at her charge with great sympathy.

Too right they can't go on like this, thought Greg and, once again, he felt the first stirrings of sensations that were already familiar to him.

It was just as Greg expected. He lost his appetite. He didn't want to move around any more. And all the comings and goings in the studio seemed to have retreated behind a curtain of mist. Even his thoughts of Sara were beginning to dissolve and become hazy. But this state of affairs was by no means as alarming as it had been the first time round.

I just have to get this one over with, Greg encouraged himself, and then I'll know what to do.

Now and then he heard Lizzie's voice. She sounded concerned, and she was doing all she could to protect him, so that he could be undisturbed. But even she couldn't prevent at least one camera being trained on him all the time.

'We're all very anxious about Greggy, dear viewers,' said Gina, speaking for once in an ordinary voice free of frantic enthusiasm. 'Many of you have called or faxed to send him good wishes for a speedy recovery. We know what a great help that is to him. And we're looking forward to having him back with us soon, fresh as ever.'

You've got a long wait coming, thought Greg wearily, his head drawn in.

'And you friends and fans of Greggy will look forward to it all the more when I tell you our plans for the near future – it'll be the event of the year! An open-air show in the Olympic stadium! Greggy will be flown in by helicopter, and all the big showbiz names will be there to welcome him. There'll be a gig with famous groups providing the mood. We'll be linked up to countless foreign transmitters. We'll be presenting an international sensation!'

Not with me, you won't, thought Greg, feeling limp

and very sleepy. I can't see what you're all on about. I'm perfectly normal. Couldn't be more normal. And once I'm fit again you can all go jump in a lake, right?

A few hours later the time came: Greg began twitching again. His skin was stretched to bursting point. The sensations were especially strong around his head, where he felt as if his mouth and jaws were cracking apart. He thought he could hear his mother's voice at a distance, speaking soothingly to him. He couldn't care less about Gina and Lizzie or anyone else watching him shed his skin this time. The important thing was to get rid of it and start a new life.

Eight

Greg's new life began with a wonderful sense of well-being. He felt fit for anything. He felt free. And he was raring to go. He thought of Sara. He also thought of Ben, and he decided that this time he was finally going to take his own fate in hand.

Lizzie was the first to turn up, bringing plenty of green stuff.

'You do look good!' she said, admiring Greg. 'I've been so worried about you.'

Nobody needs to worry about me, Greg would have liked to reply. Anyway, our ways will soon part. Thanks for looking after me, but I'm off at the next chance I get, and who knows if we'll ever meet again?

Not for the first time, Lizzie seemed to guess what Greg was thinking. She looked at him for quite a while, and then whispered, 'You know something, Greggy? I have rather a guilty conscience about all this. What they're doing to you here isn't right, and I'm seriously thinking of giving notice. If I only knew that someone else would take good care of you, or there was some other solution . . .'

Lizzie broke off in mid-sentence, and Greg felt the way he had once felt before with his mother: he knew with absolute certainty that Lizzie meant what she said. And he also picked up something else in Lizzie's mind: something she didn't want to put into words.

Soon after that Lizzie said good-night. She had left Greg with plenty of lettuce to last until morning, just as she always did.

The floodlights in the studio were dimmed to half-strength. The electronic cameras had been switched to remote control. And from somewhere or other, soft music played from a distant loudspeaker. Background music for the late-night transmission: Greggy's night life shown live, without any presenter or commentary, interrupted every twelve minutes by a long commercial break.

How am I going to get out of here? What sort of trick can you use to escape from paradise? wondered Greg, as he satisfied the appetite that had come back again. By now he knew every corner of the studio, every exit, so he also knew where he would have the best chance: there was a huge door, almost always closed, and used only when particularly large items of scenery were needed for some programme or other. Then they opened it to let in the forklift trucks, and when it was open you could hear that there was a building site outside: men were working away at top speed, constructing the Greggy Park.

Carry on, thought Greg, carry on, but you won't get *me* in that park! And as he was wondering how to escape at the next opportunity, his sensitive hearing suddenly picked up unusual sounds. First a faint crunching. Then a creaking. Then something falling to the floor.

What was that? Who was here in the studio at night? There was peace and quiet for a while, and then another slight cracking sound, footsteps, whispering – from over by the big doorway.

Greg was uneasy. His heart was thudding. He wanted to find out what was going on. Cautiously, he crawled through the artificial bushes, stopped and listened. Then he crawled on. And just as he was crawling out of a bush near the doorway, he felt something uncomfortable on his skin, impeding his movements. Something pulled and tugged at him. Short, sharp orders were issued. Then it was dark, and he picked up the disturbing sound of a car engine some-where near by. Greg felt himself being lifted in the air by forces he couldn't identify. Then there were some frantic cries close to him, and a horrible smell.

After that he lost consciousness. As he fainted, he felt he was dissolving into space, endless, boundless space, space where there was nothing . . .

Sara?

When Greg came round everything looked strange. It smelled strange too. The light wasn't what he was used to, and he immediately realised that he was restrained in some way, which was alarming.

Where am I? What happened to me? Am I still Greg the caterpillar?

He was relieved to find that he was still insatiably hungry. He was very familiar with that feeling by now. And there was plenty of green stuff lying right beside him. But this time he didn't touch it. Still dazed and rather tired, Greg turned away from the food.

What have they done to me?

It was only with difficulty that he could run the film of his memory backwards, and there were many gaps in it. That penetrating smell . . . voices, one of them bringing back memories of something quite a while ago . . . an engine, and it wasn't the first time he'd heard that either . . . the closed door . . . Ben's bedroom door . . . Sara . . .

Greg realised that several pictures which didn't really belong together were overlapping. He felt queasy.

'Come on, caterpillar, you have to eat!' a voice suddenly said beside him. 'Go on, then, eat!'

Greg obeyed. Or rather, his crunching jaws obeyed as if he had no will of his own.

As Greg munched and chewed, he tried to make out his surroundings. The floor beneath him was uncomfortably cold and smooth. All around him, in front of his wide-angled eyes, he could see nothing but bright, smooth surfaces. What about above him? It was bright there too, and there were two small holes with something inside them.

'Good, well done,' said the distorted female voice, also from above. 'I'll bring you more when you've finished.'

This is all a dream, Greg told himself.

And he was about to go on eating when a sliding door behind him opened. Several people came into the room, and with them an atmosphere of tension that immediately transferred itself to Greg.

'Well, there it is, ladies and gentlemen!'

Silence. The silence of awe and admiration.

'There's our beautiful specimen, research subject

One Double X Plus. More valuable and of more significance for the future than anything the Institute has ever seen before. Now I hope you understand why I had to encourage the powers that be to approve this spectacular operation!'

'Extraordinary!'

'Impressive!'

'Sensational!'

Greg just went on eating. Superlatives left him cold by now. But he was interested in the voice of the person presenting him with such enthusiasm. Wasn't this Dr Markstein, the mysterious biologist who'd crossed his path twice already?

'Ladies and gentlemen, any parataxonomist would envy us this world sensation. Nothing remotely like it has come into the hands of any of our colleagues recently. So let's get down to work! Our goal is Stockholm. We have no time to lose – only our reputation.'

'Stockholm? What do you mean, Doctor?' asked a woman's voice.

This caused laughter. Dr Markstein replied, in friendly tones, 'My dear girl, you should know it's the Nobel Prize we're after – the honour as well as the money. Understood?'

'Of course, Doctor.'

'One other question,' asked a male voice. 'How do we deal with the media? Abducting this creature has created a tremendous stir – it's on every news bulletin – '

'One Double X Plus instantly comes into top secret category 00. Yes, at present we are moving in an area outside the law. But the powers that be will cover up for us. Obviously, as a secret organisation themselves, our masters have already covered up a number of our other projects.'

'And what about the creature's previous owners? Will they claim it back, or how are these things arranged?' It was the woman's voice again.

'My dear girl, none of this need really concern us. One Double X Plus is in our hands, and it will stay there. I'm in amicable contact with this man Hansen, and in fact he's pleased that the big media spectacle is over. Everything else will be just a matter of money. And from now on, ladies and gentlemen, we concentrate exclusively on our scientific task. We need data, data, data! I don't need to tell you the genus of this creature, and consequently the life cycle of the species with which we are dealing. The creature's metamorphosis will follow its pre-programmed course. We don't know the exact timing, but one thing is certain: we're racing against time, and we must solve the riddle before metamorphosis occurs. Otherwise One Double X Plus will remain a one-off phenomenon, and we'll have thrown away the chance of a lifetime. So this project takes absolute priority, and now let's get down to work! I hope we shall all be successful in our experiments, and thank you for your attention.'

Soon afterwards Greg was alone again, or almost. An unerring feeling told him he was under permanent observation, even if there was nothing he could hear or smell, and no other signs of activity. He also had to absorb the news he had just heard. A good deal of it Greg simply didn't understand, but other parts of it sounded much worse than what they'd done to him in the TV studio.

Well, anyway, thought Greg, One Double X Plus had better fill the huge hole in his huge stomach to get some strength into him, and then we'll see.

There was no seeing anything much for the time being. Greg realised, gloomily, that the room was not only boringly empty, but its walls were covered with white tiles. Every time he tried crawling up them to investigate the two dark patches on the ceiling, he lost his grip and fell to the floor, which was also tiled. It was a hard landing.

'You can stop that climbing, caterpillar!' said a voice suddenly from overhead. 'Your playroom's almost ready.'

Playroom? What on earth . . . ?

But before Greg could lose his temper, a second door opened automatically with a hum, and the same voice came closer from the room next door.

'Come on, caterpillar, here's everything you need. We like to make sure all our animals are well cared for. If you want anything, that's no problem. When I'm not doing the rounds, feeding and cleaning, I sit at the monitors and watch everything. I must say you're the finest specimen that's ever found its way in here. Can't wait to see what they plan to do with you.'

Plop!

'Oh, no, I can see I'm going to have my work cut out with you!'

The animal keeper – a woman of indeterminate age, with a deep, almost masculine voice – went off, and Greg was left alone.

Over the next few hours Greg felt lonelier than he had been in a long time. There were things to investigate in the second room, but the outcome wasn't too satisfactory; its floor and walls were tiled too. Various edible offerings – lettuce, vegetables, and assorted

nibbles that smelled like guinea-pig or rabbit food –
were arranged in a series of numbered food troughs of
different colours. Still, there was a wooden climbing
frame, something to provide safe exercise. It reminded
Greg of a gorilla enclosure. Otherwise, there was
artificial light, and air-conditioning such as you get in a
plane or Intercity express. As for the dark patches on
the ceiling, one was obviously a loudspeaker and the
other the lens of a video camera – oh, great!

What have I done to deserve this? Greg tried to
work out his situation. One Double X Plus was feeling
very cross indeed, and urgently needed some bright
ideas. Urgently!

Had days passed, or only hours? Was it day or night at
this moment?

How come I've lost my sense of time? Greg
wondered, when he heard the electronic door opening
again after what seemed an eternity. At least he
recognised Dr Markstein's voice.

'As I have told you, it must be handled only with the
utmost caution! This creature is not to be injured, and it
must not fall ill. Furthermore, in so far as it is possible
for such creatures to do so, it must be persuaded to trust
us. Psychopharmaceuticals such as we have used in the
past, mind-bending drugs, must be kept to the absolute

minimum dosage and increased only in an emergency, for fear of affecting the results of our laboratory experiments. And now, if you please, straight to the CT department!'

Once again, Greg understood only about half of this. He felt himself being lifted by a number of hands and some indefinable, humming mechanical device, and automatically steered to a flat surface. Here, assorted plastic grips secured his whole body. Then he was wheeled out and down a long corridor that went on for ever.

What are they doing to me? What's that horrible squealing and squeaking? Why don't I defend myself? Why do I feel so limp? What are all the smells in this building?

Soon afterwards, Greg found himself in a brightly illuminated room. He heard brief orders being given in a language where almost every other word was foreign to him. And just as he had decided not to put up with this any more, he was suddenly placed inside a narrow tunnel. Mysterious, alarming darkness surrounded him. He heard voices as strange, muffled sounds. Greg was scared. Badly scared. He wanted to get out of this position, emerge from the dark tunnel – but he was strapped down, restrained by something holding each of his segments in place and making movement impossible. From a distance, he heard first a humming, then a squeaking, and then, very far off, the voices again. They were matter-of-fact at first, becoming more and more excited.

'No! I don't believe it!'

'Look at that!'

'The heart!'

'Is that the physiology of a normal caterpillar you have before you? See the difference? Take a good look, my dear colleagues!'

Greg couldn't see anything himself, because it was pitch dark. He couldn't understand anything either. Clearly they were looking at parts of his insides, and he thought that in itself was unpleasant. Also, he was cramped in here, and hungry, and . . . and . . .

'And here we have the genital area! Take a look at that screen: yes, sexual organs indisputably male. That in itself takes us an important step further!'

Oh, very interesting! Sexual organs indisputably male . . .

Then Greg was free. It was light again. Someone put green leaves in front of his jaws, but Greg didn't feel well. Although his stomach was grumbling with hunger, he refused the leaves.

I don't want any more of this! I've had it up to here! Can't you understand that?

* * *

When Greg was back where it seemed he had to spend his time at present, a chaotic series of images was whirling through his mind: audiocassettes, video-cassettes, Ben's door, the big studio door, genital areas, computer parts, jelly babies, lettuces, and a huge, crowded bus where he kept looking in vain for Sara . . .

Come on, Greg, pull yourself together, don't let them get you down! You must keep a clear head, Greg! How come you didn't escape from home? Or that studio? Why won't anyone help you? Don't they realise you're not a normal caterpillar? Yes, but how are you to make them understand that when you can't talk?

Then came the surprise. At first Greg didn't trust his hearing, good as it was. But then he smelled her. The animal keeper had brought his mother into the room.

'Here, Mrs Hansen, see for yourself. We're keeping it in the most hygienic of conditions, with exactly the diet it needs. It has plenty of space for exercise. It can climb and play as if it were in the wild.'

'But this looks just like the – '

'I'm not the person to complain to,' said the keeper, interrupting Mrs Hansen. 'You'll have to write to the management of the Institute if you want to complain.'

'Greggy!'

Greg was confused. Yes, this woman was

Mrs Hansen. He knew her very well. But who was he? What did this Mrs Hansen want with him?

'Can you hear me, Greg? Do you know me? Are you feeling all right?'

'Nnnn . . . nnn . . . chchch . . .'

For the first time in ages, and involuntarily, Greg managed to make a few sounds again. It was a great effort.

'Greg, we just don't know what to do. We're all under dreadful strain. And yesterday Grandfather . . .'

Mrs Hansen stopped, tears running down her cheeks, and stared helplessly at the caterpillar.

'Don't you worry, Mrs Hansen. It's a bit temperamental, that's all. But it's eating regularly and getting the best of veterinary care.'

'He's not well. I can see he isn't. I – oh, I can't stand it any longer!'

Greg stayed on the floor, not moving. His segments felt numb, and it was taking him much longer than usual to convey outside impressions to his mind.

Yes, that was his mother. The caterpillar's mother. Ben's mother. And what about Grandfather? Yesterday Grandfather did what?

It was some time after Mrs Hansen had left the Institute before Greg realised what she had begun telling him about Grandfather.

* * *

'Ladies and gentlemen of the media, please assure yourselves that this creature is very well cared for here. As we expected, or feared, or hoped – whichever you like – this is not a normal caterpillar. And I don't mean just its size: I mean its physiology. Preliminary investigations in our laboratory indicate an extra-ordinary biological phenomenon. We have yet to explore the background and the entire context.'

Greg heard Dr Markstein's voice coming over the loudspeaker in the ceiling. He was still trying to work out what kind of meeting or conference was going on.

'Ladies and gentlemen, I can well understand that you would like to see Greggy at close quarters, but I must ask for your forbearance. In this case, science comes first. Our Institute is working not for its own ends, but with a sense of responsibility to society as a whole, to all of you. Genetic engineering will help to solve our health problems. Genetic engineering will help to create new chances of survival and a new quality of life in this new millennium. And we can succeed in these aims only if we have your trust and support. Please leave us alone to work in peace, and all of us, including the creature entrusted to our care, will be grateful to you.'

* * *

He didn't have to wait long for the next set of examinations. One of them had the whole Institute in an uproar.

'Sensational! Look at these ultrasound pictures. What do you see there, colleagues? A human brain! A brain identical to that of a human being! Now do you know what we're working on?'

What's the matter with them? I could have told them that straight off, thought Greg, amused, although there were no real grounds for him to feel any amusement.

Once again, several people came into Greg's room, and of course Dr Markstein was among them.

'Now, look at this creature. Imagine having several specimens of this kind in the near future! For that's our aim, and we must pursue it by every possible means. Dolly the sheep pales by comparison – a minor and insignificant experiment in cloning. So let's get down to work!'

Greg was lying coiled up in a corner near the feeding troughs. His head had been clearer for the last few hours. His thoughts were getting more logically organised again. And he had already made a decision: I'm going to resist anything they try doing to me. I'm not putting up with this any more!

'Where exactly do we take the tissue samples from, Doctor?'

Tissue samples? Greg's cornicle came up in the air. His alarming camouflage face was on show. The stinging hairs stood out threateningly from his body, although he felt ridiculously helpless with only them as weapons.

'You can stimulate that cornicle if you like – we need some of its secretions too.'

Greg felt someone touching his back segment, and was overcome by furious rage. What business do they have fumbling about with me? I'll sting them! I'll sting them so badly they won't dare come near me.

'There – you can wipe it off the cornicle now.'

Greg realised how helpless he really was. If he came out of his protective position they could even get at his head, and he was more scared of that than anything else.

'Now to take samples from all parts of the body. You take one from the hind legs, please, you from the skin, and we'll tackle the front segments . . . careful!'

As Greg felt the pricks and little cuts he began to struggle more violently than he had ever done except when shedding his skin. As if automatically, his head shot out.

'Don't use force!' said Dr Markstein. 'Well, obviously we can do this only under anaesthetic.'

Anaesthetic?

Beside himself, Greg reared up and tried to get at

Dr Markstein. His jaws were trembling. His bright red cornicle gave off an unpleasant smell. His head was tense to the point of bursting. It was the men on Dr Markstein's team rather than the women scientists who laughed at his efforts.

'Look at the little fellow!'

'Nature certainly takes some strange paths.'

'Leave the poor creature alone. Let's give him an injection.'

Injection!

Greg twitched. He wanted to make a break for it, but several pairs of hands grabbed his front legs. He felt two painful pricks at the back of his head, and then he lost consciousness.

'I'm sorry, Gregor, but we had no choice,' he heard his father whispering, somewhere close. 'We always warned you, didn't we? If you hadn't watched so many wildlife films, if you'd concentrated more at school, if you didn't have so many daft ideas in your head, if you hadn't gone off the rails, if you hadn't done this, if you hadn't done that, if you hadn't . . .'

'I want to talk again!' Greg heard himself saying.

'And I know who to, who to, who to,' whispered Ben. 'Want me to tell Dr Markstein you stole that cassette from my room? Want me to give you away to everyone here in Paradise, in Paradise?'

'This isn't Paradise, Ben, this is Hell. Only you don't notice because you never talk to me, little brother!'

'Did you call *me* little brother, Greggy? *Did* you?'

'Yes, I did. Little brother, little brother, little brother.'

'Oh terrific, baby brother, very clever, I must say!'

'Yes, it is, it is, it is . . .'

When Greg slowly came back to his senses he had considerable difficulty standing on his many pairs of legs. He urgently wanted to open a pair of human eyes and see everything plain and clear. He could tell by the smell that he was in his quarters, his private double cell, but at the same time the smell of the laboratories where he had spent the last few hours clung to him.

'You must eat, you must eat plenty, caterpillar!' said a voice from the ceiling loudspeakers.

Greg felt like shouting: I'm not having you tell me what to do!

'If you don't eat of your own accord we'll have to try artificial feeding.'

Artificial feeding? Are they mad?

'Did you understand, caterpillar?'

Am I really a caterpillar? Greg asked himself, and at that moment he had a very strange experience: the old, two-legged, thinking Greg came apart from the caterpillar body with all its segments, just left it behind and floated up to the ceiling. He stayed up there beside the video eye, turned, and looked down on the giant caterpillar with great interest.

'What's the matter with you, caterpillar?' asked the loudspeaker.

I'm looking at myself, Greg signalled to the unpleasantly intrusive voice next to him, and you just keep out of this!

And as he looked down on himself he thought: you know, that caterpillar is impressive, really impressive! No wonder he's hungry all the time. He probably just has to grow a bit more, and then . . .

There was a pitiful squeaking from outside, and all of a sudden Greg stopped hovering. His mind was back in the caterpillar body, and he was aware of his giant stomach again.

Greg, you must eat. Eat plenty. It's your only chance. You must grow a bit more, and then . . .

Greg did as he had told himself. He ordered his back pair of legs to crawl over to the feeding troughs . . . second pair, third pair . . . going a little further forward all the time. At last he was enjoying this movement again.

I'm going to eat and eat and eat, and then . . .

Like a caterpillar possessed, Greg abandoned himself to his appetite, and then, over the next few days, as if in a numbed state, he let them do things to him that he didn't really like at all. He was weighed and measured. More tissue, skin and body fluid samples were taken. His movements were observed and recorded, his eating patterns were dissected, even his droppings were carefully collected and removed for analysis.

Only when they started talking about some important visit did Greg take notice again. Had he heard the name Auster?

It turned out that Sara's father was there because he was a solicitor.

'Mr Auster, we really have nothing to hide. We can meet any legal investigation with perfect confidence. But please convince yourself in person of the creature's well-being.'

That was Dr Markstein's voice. Next moment the sliding door opened, and Greg heard someone come in.

'Would you like to be left alone with him?'

'Yes, please.'

That smell! It was almost like Sara's . . .

And that voice! Quite different from Sara's, yet there was something in the sound of it that made Greg so excited he could hardly bear it.

'Well, how are you?'

Greg's heart was thudding. He felt excited, and shy, and he wanted to crawl away and hide somewhere.

'I suppose this is the most unusual visit I've ever paid to a client,' said Mr Auster.

He's excited too, thought Greg, listening intently.

'I'm here on behalf of Sara.'

Mr Auster was standing straight in front of Greg, who could sense his closeness, his warmth, his smell, and something else . . .

'I'm to give you her very best wishes, and bring you this to keep your strength up. It's from a ginkgo.'

A ginkgo?

'A tree species 250 million years old. Unique on the planet, with special healing powers. Sara said you'd know about it.'

Something 250 million years old . . .

???

Mr Auster put a small leafy twig down in front of Greg's jaws.

'There we are, then. I imagine a visit now and then would be good for you, right? And a personal nurse seems to me a good notion, too. I'll see about it, shall I?'

Greg didn't move. This was like a dream. If he moved now there might be a pop, and the giant balloon of his dream would burst.

But there was no pop (and no plop either). Mr Auster disappeared. The door closed. Greg absorbed the smell left behind by Sara's father, soaking it up through all his pores. And then he was overcome by a desire to get Sara's present well and truly inside him.

'Stop! No!' cried the voice from the loudspeaker. 'You mustn't eat that. You must have the prescribed diet and nothing else.'

You just try stopping me! What do you know, any of you?

And Greg set about happily eating the ginkgo leaves.

However, his pleasure was short lived. The next few days were horrible. Dr Markstein and his team seemed to be in a very nervous state. They kept making new observations and doing more examinations. There was talk of electrocardiograms and radiocardiographs, ultrasound diagnoses and scintigraphies. Results were exchanged and compared. There was much discussion, and mysterious plans were drawn up.

'If we don't get the decoding finished in time we'll have no option,' announced Dr Markstein. 'Before he goes and metamorphoses on us we'll have to put him on ice, literally. I'd prefer to avoid the procedure, but it's the lesser risk. Get everything ready for that even-tuality, and at the first sign of metamorphosis we act.'

Put me on ice?

Greg didn't have much time to think about that. A

special examination of him was arranged, and once again he had no chance to defend himself. One of the scientists came up behind him as he was in a resting position and gave him an injection in the back to keep him quiet.

I'm never going to draw my head in again, Greg decided, before his senses faded, and he felt the rest of what happened only hazily.

He was taken to a special lab, where special apparatus was waiting for him. 'He's staying here until we know all about his brain,' Dr Markstein announced. 'Give him infusions as soon as his condition becomes unstable. I need an EEG of all his waking, sleeping and particularly dreaming phases. I need precise images of both hemispheres of the brain. We want his condition at present, but we want his past too. I want information about his dreaming so that I can project the future. You understand what I'm asking you to do?'

He's deranged. Out of his mind! This realisation formed in Greg's mind very slowly, surrounded by other and even vaguer perceptions. I'd like this Markstein . . . this so-and-so Markstein . . . I'd like him to know what Greg . . . what Gregor Hansen . . . I'd like him to know what I think of him . . . think of him, think of him . . .

* * *

In his semiconscious state, Greg was aware not just of confusing, crazy ideas. No less confusing were first a familiar smell, then a name he thought he heard.

'Here's your friend, Mrs Land. Yes, we have tried to dissuade the Hansen family's legal adviser from this idea, but we have nothing to hide. Our research is dedicated to promoting the welfare of mankind, and that, of course, means the welfare of the animal kingdom too. As long as you don't get in the way of our investigations you're welcome to look after our fascinating specimen. Perhaps it will make our work easier.'

Land?

'Greg?'

Lizzie!

'Greggy, can you hear me?'

Greg couldn't hear much, but enough. Before he lost consciousness entirely, one thought became a certainty: I'm going to make it.

When Greg came round again after a long, long dream journey, he was certainly back in his cell, but Lizzie was really there with him.

'Greg, you're not on your own any more. I'm going to look after you from now on.'

'Make sure you feed him, please,' said the voice from the loudspeaker.

'I know how to treat him, thank you,' said Lizzie to the video camera. 'Please keep out of this.'

'Huh! You wouldn't dare speak to Dr Markstein in those tones!'

Lizzie seemed to ignore this remark. She leaned down to Greg and whispered urgently, 'Listen, my dear! I'm here to help you. I've had a long conversation with this Markstein. I knew him already. An expert in his field, but a fanatic too. If I've guessed his plans correctly, he's intending to do something with you that I won't allow. Can you understand any of what I'm saying?'

Greg moved closer to Lizzie, hoping she would take that as an answer.

'I've been in this Institute before. In fact, I worked here twice. Once they get something into their laboratories they don't let it out again. There are influential economists supporting the place, and important politicians protecting it. Now, you must trust me implicitly, or you'll never get out either.'

'Mrs Land, would you please come straight to my office? I'd like a little talk.' It was Dr Markstein's voice, sounding arrogant and cold.

'Eat up, Greggy,' said Lizzie softly. 'Eat to keep your

strength up. I'll be back as soon as I can.'

'You've got visitors, caterpillar!'

This time it wasn't Lizzie, but two male figures. They entered the room. The sliding door closed behind them, humming, and there was silence.

Go on eating, just go on eating, Greg told himself, but he was confused. There was a smell of building sites, of computers, of jelly babies.

'Hey, you there!'

'Hallo, Greg!'

Ben and Pa!

Greg turned slowly, very slowly, away from his bowl of lettuce. The front of his body was reared up, and as usual he could make out only the dark outline of someone standing close to him.

'Wow, has he ever grown!' he heard Ben saying.

'We wanted to see how you were,' said Mr Hansen. 'I'm worried. I want to help you.'

Greg didn't move, but deep down inside he began to tremble.

'As a lawyer, Auster managed to get Lizzie taken on to look after you. Look, I'm really sorry about all this. So many things have turned out wrong.'

What on earth is all this? I'm not used to Pa in this mood!

Greg's trembling got worse. He could barely hide it.

'Hey, I brought you something,' said Ben, coming close to Greg. 'You like these, right?'

He was holding a bag of outsize jelly babies in front of Greg's feelers.

'Come on, eat this!'

Greg didn't want to. His body was twitching, and at the same time he felt paralysed by having his brother so close.

'Go on,' whispered Ben urgently. 'Eat it at once, and for heaven's sake don't throw it up again!'

'Listen to what Ben's telling you!' urged Mr Hansen too. 'It's for your own good.'

Greg heard the words, and he could feel how agitated Ben and his father were, but at the same time his insides seemed to constrict, and he couldn't understand what they wanted.

'Oh, for goodness' sake, open your mouth and swallow this!' whispered Ben, pushing something small and hard between his jaws.

There was a humming noise, and the sliding door opened.

'It's a mini transmitter, Greg, get the idea?'

'Please don't touch the caterpillar!' said the voice of the woman keeper. 'This is a very sensitive animal and doesn't like being disturbed.'

Greg swallowed.

'Okay, well done!' said Ben.

Greg swallowed once more.

'We'll come and see you again. Good luck,' said Mr Hansen.

Greg swallowed for the third time, and almost retched, and then the mini transmitter went down. Twitching and wriggling, he dropped his front segments to the floor as his father and Ben disappeared.

'Just as I feared!'

A little later, there stood Dr Markstein with the senior members of his team, looking at the wriggling caterpillar.

'We must act at once. It'll need an injection before the acute stage of skin-shedding begins,' someone said.

'Or before it pupates, my dear fellow!' said Dr Markstein.

'But you can't *do* that – you can't stop the process!' protested Lizzie.

'You are here as an animal keeper, not an anesthetist, Mrs Land. I will ask you to keep out of this, or I'll have to take the necessary steps.'

His words were as sharp and hurtful to Greg as the injection a moment later.

'Now to tranquillise it,' someone said.

Greg was still trembling.

'Do we put it in the pre-cooling chamber at once?'

'No, first we must check the instruments,' said Dr Markstein. He sounded nervous. 'Nothing must go wrong this time.'

'What about the press conference?'

'Cancel it! Say he's severely ill. The next press release will be after he's frozen. Not a word earlier. Not even to our masters, right? We must present them with a deep-frozen *fait accompli*.'

Pre-cooling chamber . . . frozen . . . deep-frozen *fait accompli*? Greg didn't want to think any more. Greg *couldn't* think any more.

A little later he was perfectly calm. The attacks of wriggling had stopped. His appetite had entirely disappeared. The smell of Lizzie beside him was pleasant, but nothing really seemed to matter – Greg just wanted to dream. He wanted to dream he was dreaming, and maybe this nightmare would come to an end some time . . . .

'Listen, my dear,' Lizzie whispered. 'Don't be afraid. It's going to be cold for you soon. Very cold, but I'll be there with you, and when night comes it will all be over.'

Greg felt as if he were drugged as they took him to

the pre-cooling chamber of the Institute. He could make out only patterns of light – light and dark, and something red here and there. The noises were unclear too – now and then a sound like something barking, or squealing, or squeaking in the distance, and then silence again, silence lulling him to sleep.

'I hope you're warmly dressed, Mrs Land,' said Dr Markstein, sarcastically, as the stretcher party stopped outside a large aluminium door.

'Thank you for your concern.'

'It may get too cold for you towards morning, Mrs Land. You can safely leave the rest of the procedure to us. Of course, we'll inform you when we defrost him again. As far as I can see, looking at our timetable, we'll need a maximum six months for our research. An annoying delay, but even scientists are only human.'

'I quite see that,' said Lizzie.

The electronic door opening device hummed, and Greg was taken into a room so cold that every breath and every word condensed into a wisp of mist.

'Here, the remote control for when it gets too cold for you, Mrs Land. We're only equipped to experiment on animals. Good-night.'

Dr Markstein's smile was an icy one itself. The door automatically closed.

Greg and Lizzie were alone.

'You have to hold out, Greggy! Please hold out!'

Lizzie kept trying to prevent Greg from going to sleep. She stroked his back to slow down the cooling process. She tickled, scratched and massaged him, trying to get him to keep moving.

Yes, okay, thought Greg wearily, but he kept lapsing back into that twilight condition, feeling as if he had to walk or hover through some region between worlds.

'Please hold out till midnight, Greggy. That's when they're going to come and take you away.'

To Paradise ... to the Greggy Paradise ... the caterpillar dreamed he was back in the TV studio.

'Hi there, Greggy fans ... hi there, powers that be ... hi, Ben fans ... here, today, we present our deep-frozen toilet ... luscious caterpillar meat from the firm of Markstein One Double X Plus, freshly served on the table ... grotesque, gregoresque, telephonesque ...' For the mobile in Lizzie's jacket pocket had just bleeped.

'Yes?'

Greg had woken up slightly. He thought he knew the voice on the phone.

'Everything going to plan?'

'So far. I'm waiting till just before midnight. The waste disposal men never come before one a.m. If they have any of the Institute people with them you'll need to be careful. How long is the transmitter's range?'

'At least a thousand metres.'

'That should do. Don't take any risks – this lot won't shrink from a confrontation.'

Nor me . . . nor me, thought Greg, before dreaming himself back in his Greggy Park.

'And today Gina . . . Gina . . . Gina presents the powers that be in opera . . . grand opera . . . grand operation: chasing Greggy, Greggy's on the run with Dolly . . . live on the run . . . mad about Dolly . . .'

Her name's Sara, thought Greg, trying to clear this point up, but his consciousness was fading once again.

It was midnight when Lizzie used the remote control to get out of the pre-cooling chamber. She ran along the basement corridor as fast as she could. Then she stopped outside a door with a notice on it saying Toxic Waste, and the nuclear sign, and she listened. She knew that around this time of night the Institute was dead to the world, particularly on a Friday.

'Come on, Lizzie, nothing's going to happen to you!'

Alarmed by the sound of her own voice, Lizzie turned around.

Then everything happened very fast: she opened the door with the remote control. Put an empty container on the trolley. Close the door, back to Greggy. Open the door, trolley in, close the door.

'Greg! Greggy, you must move!'

Lizzie tapped the caterpillar, slapped his back, tried to shake him. 'Listen, you must get in here!'

Greg heard something, and felt something. He felt sick. He felt like throwing up. Deep inside him there were pictures, and words . . . and something indigestible made of metal.

'Come *on*, Greggy! In this container!'

Retching . . . pain . . . Greg tried to throw up.

'No, no, please don't, or they won't find you!'

At that moment there was a sound, a hum . . . the door opened, and there stood the woman keeper.

'Scuse me, just wondered if you'd like a nice cup of tea?'

'Thanks, I – '

'What's the matter? Problems with that caterpillar?'

'He's been contaminated. He must be got out of here.'

'Where to?'

'Never mind that, just help me!'

'You mean he's going to the waste dump?'

'Yes.'

'But the doctor said . . .'

'Help me, can't you!'

'Will you take the responsibility, then?'

'*Yes.*'

'Okay, I'll help.'

Greg felt two pairs of hands pushing him, shoving him, trying to lift him.

'Get in here! Then you can sleep all you like until the injection wears off.'

I'll do it, said Greg to himself with the last of his strength, and then everything went dark around him.

Half an hour later, the van appeared in the court-yard of the Institute to take away toxic waste. Without a word, men in protective clothing did what they did every Friday, unloading empty containers, rolling the full containers of waste up from the basement, loading them into the van. A brief good-night to the night porter. Start the engine, drive off, drive away ... problem dealt with.

Greg woke up just before dawn. He was somewhere dark and cramped. Poisonous vapours were practically suffocating him.

Where am I?

There was a painful thudding in Greg's head. His whole body was sore. Also he still felt nausea.

What's happened?

He tried to move, and was surprised to find his segments weren't so stiff any more.

Lizzie?

Greg tried to get his bearings, but the sharp, acrid smells made it difficult.

Have they poisoned me? What was it Grandfather said? That story by the writer called Kafka, and the man in it called Gregor perished miserably?

What was it he'd said? Go your way, your own personal way, and don't let anyone stop you – remember that.

Well, I did remember it. But I do feel dreadful ... I have to get out of here ... I have to get away from here.

No problem about that. Greg just had to stretch and rear up, and the lid over him lifted of its own accord.

Air, fresh air! thought Greg, but immediately his whole body contracted with nausea. Evil-smelling vapours were drifting over him, acrid fogs hurt his eyes ... with determination, Greg did something he hadn't succeeded in doing for ages. He pushed himself forward and up and over the edge of the container.

Now what?

All Greg could make out in the dim light were confused outlines. It was deathly still.

If I don't get away from here at once, I'll die too ... Yes, go your own way, said Greg to himself sternly, but then he retched again. Go on, eat that at once and don't bring it up again! Ben's words mingled with the poisonous smells . . . I'm to bring you this ginkgo to get your strength up. Please, prayed Greg as he threw up, just the mini transmitter, not the ginkgo leaves!

Greg felt empty. Very empty.

It was ages since he'd eaten, but he didn't feel hungry. Things felt sharp under his feet: sharp edges, broken glass, splinters. And he hardly dared move in this desert of disgusting rubbish.

Where's the way out? Where's there a path?

As Greg helplessly tried to orientate himself, he suddenly heard sirens – in the distance, but rapidly coming closer.

A flashing blue light mingled with the red sky of dawn.

They're after me! thought Greg. They're looking for me! Suddenly he was wide awake.

They're not going to catch up with me at this late stage!

He set off, his mind made up, cautiously putting foot in front of foot in search of ground that wouldn't injure him. He tried to distribute his weight so that each step would be as short and take as little weight as possible.

An idea shot through his head. You're an animal,

and animals have instincts. Let your instinct look for the safest way to get away from those horrible sirens.

So he moved on with caterpillar skill, step by step, while the evil-smelling mists almost deprived him of the air he needed to survive.

Sara! The thought of Sara gave Greg courage. Sara sent me those leaves, and now they must show me the way.

Was it these thoughts, or the fear of his pursuers, or just the course of his story that saved Greg?

At some point, he found himself facing a wall that no human being could have climbed.

So why am I a caterpillar? he asked himself, crawling nimbly up it with his many legs. Briefly, he stopped to enjoy being so high up, and then, as the sound of the sirens died away rapidly in the distance, he climbed down to the other side.

He was tired, so tired! Caterpillars lead lives of endless stress, thought Greg, wishing he could lie down on the spot.

Endless stress? Really endless?

No, there's an end somewhere, thought Greg, and after a long time his feelers moved again . . .

By giving up thought altogether, leaving himself just a creature that had to find its way, Greg found a place where he could stay for a while. He felt both restless and at peace. He just had to give way to an impulse that seemed to come to him of itself.

There was a tree ahead of him, a tree with a familiar smell. It was easy to climb its trunk, and he immediately found a nice quiet place. Now he had only to spin, spin, go on spinning, spin himself a cocoon and wait patiently. Dreaming, dreaming and . . .

Greg had a delightful dream. His body changed, and he didn't need to do anything about it. First it changed down at the end, where he could move his toes and count them. Then it changed up his legs, to the place that was sometimes so familiar and sometimes so infuriatingly unreliable . . . and went on to his stomach, his chest, his shoulders . . . The sense of metamorphosis became better and better: he had arms, he had hands . . . he could move all his fingers . . . he had fingers for writing with, painting with, holding things, stroking things.

The metamorphosis, Greg noticed, wasn't over yet. He had something to hold his head up now, something other than the branch where he was resting . . . he had a neck, and a throat which could make sounds . . . at first just dream sounds accompanying the dream images forming before his eyes, which were new but still closed.

'Hey, where are you, then?'

Am I awake, or am I dreaming?

'Sorry I'm a bit late.'

Late? What was the problem?

'Want me to come up to you, or will you come down
to me?'

Up, down? Down, up? Meet in the middle, maybe?

'Come on, open your eyes! Have you been waiting
for me long?'

Well, that was the question . . . depended how you
looked at it, right?

Anyway, Greg couldn't have cared less. His heart
was thudding. It had been thudding ever since she first
said, 'Hey'.

He had other feelings too, and if he stopped to think
about it he supposed he didn't stand a chance. But he
opened his eyes, looked straight into Sara's, and grinned
widely with delight, and pleasure, and high spirits.

'Yes!' he shouted.

'Yes what?'

'Yes to the question on your cassette!' cried Greg,
and with a huge leap he jumped down from the tree
and landed right in front of Sara.

'So now?'

So now?